**"I wish**
**wake up together.**

Luke was shocked to hear himself. "Uh...I mean..."

"Yes," Darcy breathed, "I know what you mean."

Their lips met in a long, deep kiss that made him aware of every square inch of their bodies that were touching.

"Whatever happens," she said when their lips parted, "you know it's only temporary."

"I know." He kissed her again.

"I can't stay."

His mouth moved against hers as he murmured, "I know that, too."

Their gazes met. "I don't want any sad scenes when I have to leave," Darcy said.

It was something he could promise now, but what about in two weeks? What if they did finally make love and it was as wonderful as he imagined? Would he be able to let her go?

Dear Reader,

We hope that, like Kathy Clark, you'll take a moment to *Count Your Blessings* this Thanksgiving. Those of us at Harlequin sure are grateful to you, our readers, for making this year's CALENDAR OF ROMANCE promotion such a success.

Next month, we'll be celebrating Christmas by bringing you a present of not one, but *four*, CALENDAR OF ROMANCE titles. All themed around the magic and wonder that is the holiday season. There's even one book about Hanukkah, the Festival of Lights, that we're sure you'll enjoy.

Join us next month for our tribute to the last—and the best—of all the holidays!

As always, we welcome your comments on the CALENDAR OF ROMANCE. Write to us at the address below.

Sincerely,

Debra Matteucci
Senior Editor & Editorial Coordinator
Harlequin Books
300 East 42nd St., 6th floor
New York, NY 10017

# KATHY CLARK

## COUNT YOUR BLESSINGS

# *Harlequin Books*

TORONTO • NEW YORK • LONDON
AMSTERDAM • PARIS • SYDNEY • HAMBURG
STOCKHOLM • ATHENS • TOKYO • MILAN
MADRID • WARSAW • BUDAPEST • AUCKLAND

This book is dedicated to my own Greg, Adam and Scott. Thanks for the inspiration. I count my blessings everyday because you three are my sons.

Published November 1992

ISBN 0-373-16461-5

COUNT YOUR BLESSINGS

# Chapter One

"Sometimes it seems like nothing's going right in your life. But you should stop feeling sorry for yourself and count your blessings. Remember, the Lord works in mysterious ways...."

The minister's sermon continued, but Darcy's attention wandered to the blaze of autumn color outside the church's tall, arched windows. A breeze, brisk with the promise of winter, persistently plucked the leaves from the trees and sent them swirling to the ground.

The distinct changing of the seasons was one of the few things she missed since she moved to California. There was something invigorating about the crispness of fall and something reassuring about the rebirth of spring. But for Darcy, spring seemed light-years away.

How had she let herself get so caught up in the race for TV ratings? She knew she had been dancing on the boundaries of legality. But she hadn't, for a second, believed she'd get caught. Not Darcy Carson. She was too careful, too professional, too important.

How was the station getting along without her? Was it wishful thinking that the viewing audience would miss her? Or, realistically, would her job still be there after her case made it through the court system?

An apprehensive shiver slipped through her confident armor, and it took several seconds for her to swallow back the panic that rose in her throat. *Calm down, Darcy,* she silently admonished. *You're going to get through this and be back in front of the cameras by the first of November.*

*But what if you aren't?* that annoying little voice in her head kept repeating. *Not only could your career be over, but you could find out what a jail cell looks like from the inside.*

Something sharp jabbed her neck, and she swatted it away. A tiny silver airplane drifted to a perfect landing on the skirt of her forest green wool suit. Darcy picked up the triangular-shaped craft and studied its construction with experienced eyes. Fashioned from the lining of a stick of gum, she could smell the distinctive Juicy Fruit fragrance clinging to the foil. She and her brothers had folded many similar planes during the Sunday services of their youth until her parents would notice the mini-air battles and make confiscation attacks that quickly ended the wars.

Darcy slid a surreptitious glance at the row behind her and immediately identified the guilty aviators. Three boys, ranging from elementary school to high school age sat, their hands folded neatly in their laps, their clean-scrubbed faces staring at the minister as if he were reciting the opening passages of the latest "Star Trek" episode instead of expounding on the scriptures.

Seated next to the youngest boy, an elderly woman was looking toward the front, genuinely paying attention to the sermon and totally oblivious to the children's activities.

Darcy smiled. She hadn't been to this church for almost twelve years. Since then *real* wars had been fought and won, women's hemlines had gone down to their ankles and back up to their thighs, and the stock market had broken three thousand. And yet, in this old-fashioned church nestled in a grove of ancient oak trees, very little had changed. Almost the entire population of Greenhaven still showed up for Sunday morning services. And while the adults listened to the sermon, the children did anything they could think of not to.

Just as Darcy was looking away, the littlest boy's gaze wandered, turning to meet hers with an irresistible blend of mischief and innocence in his big blue eyes. He flashed her a grin that earned him a sharp poke in his ribs from his brother's elbow.

Darcy's mother, Betty, reached over and rested her hand on her daughter's arm. Darcy looked down at the wrinkled, callused fingers and covered them with her own. It was funny how, regardless of her age, the touch of her mother's hand reduced Darcy to a time when her whole world had been in this small corner of Iowa. That was one of the reasons she had left. She had wanted to get away so she could grow up and stand on her own two feet. But now, with her career teetering on the edge, it felt good to be home with her family. Here, with her mother and father sitting on one side of her and her two brothers and their families on the other, Darcy was insulated from the real world. At least for a few days.

After the closing prayer, Darcy stood with the rest of the congregation and was immediately surrounded by her family and old acquaintances.

"Darcy, dear," her mother said. "I want you to meet our new neighbor, Nell. Her son bought the old Willowby place down by the lake."

The woman standing next to Betty smiled and extended her hand. "Betty never stops talking about you," she said to Darcy.

"Then I apologize," Darcy responded with a laugh as she shook Nell's hand. "That must get pretty boring."

"Of course it doesn't," Nell denied. "Working in television must be fascinating."

"I love it," Darcy agreed.

The young boy with the big blue eyes wiggled his way through the crowd and tugged on Nell's skirt. "Daddy says we need to leave. He's waiting outside." He looked up at Darcy and flashed her a hesitant grin. "Hi."

She gave him a conspiratorial wink. "Hi. My name's Darcy. What's yours?"

"Scott," he answered. Already there was a smudge of dirt across his chin and one side of his shirttail had come untucked.

"Nice to meet you, Scott. Were those your brothers sitting with you?"

He grimaced and nodded.

Before Darcy could continue the conversation, Nell took Scott's hand. "I guess we'd better get going. It's our busy time of year at the farm, you know."

Everyone nodded their agreement as if they did, indeed, understand.

It wasn't until Darcy was helping her mother prepare lunch that she had a chance to ask what sort of crop the Calloways raised.

"Oh, they don't actually grow crops," Betty explained as she stirred flour and milk into the chicken broth to make gravy. "They raise turkeys."

"Turkeys!" Darcy's nose wrinkled as if one of the birds had just walked into the room. "I remember the year we raised turkeys for 4-H. They're noisy, stinky, stupid creatures."

"Well, someone has to do it or we wouldn't have turkey for Thanksgiving, would we?" Betty replied with unquestionable logic.

"Maybe so," Darcy acknowledged. "But thank goodness his farm is downwind."

"Just think, Darce," her older brother Bob teased, "if you hadn't left when you did, you could have married a farmer and had a flock of your own."

"A flock of what...kids or turkeys?" Bob's wife Sue asked.

"As far as Darcy's concerned, there's no difference between the two." Bob laughed. "They're both noisy and stinky."

"Bob!" his mother and his wife exclaimed simultaneously.

Bob cast a pointed look at Darcy. "I don't hear any denials from you."

"And you won't." She wiped imaginary perspiration off her forehead and sighed dramatically. "But for the grace of God I'd be stuck out there feeding animals, kids and a hayseed husband."

"Darcy!" Betty admonished. "Don't blaspheme."

"Yeah, Darcy," her younger brother Steven echoed. "Being a turkey farmer's wife isn't glamorous like being a famous television star."

"Being a TV journalist isn't all that glamorous, either," Darcy retorted. "But at least the only mouth I have to feed is my own."

"Speaking of which," Bob interrupted as he edged toward a platter piled high with crispy fried chicken, "when can I expect my mouth to be fed? The football game starts in less than an hour."

Darcy twisted the dish towel and snapped it toward him, deftly flicking his hand. "See, that's two more reasons I haven't gotten married."

Betty clicked her tongue and shook her head. "I still have hope that someday you'll meet a wonderful man and settle down."

"I *am* settled down, Mother." Darcy slipped her arms around Betty's still slender waist. "I have a very nice house in Santa Monica. If you'd ever come out for a visit, you'd see that my life-style is pretty normal. I even have flower boxes and a couple of orange trees in the backyard."

Betty's response was emphatic. "No thanks. I don't want an earthquake to bury me while I'm sleeping."

"I've lived there for six years and the worst damage I've had is when a coffee cup shook off the table and cut my foot."

"Well, I'll just stay here in our peaceful corner of the world and live happily with my husband on our little farm...."

Darcy rolled her eyes and laughed. "You need to work on your subtlety, Mother."

"Okay, then I'll be blunt. You're thirty-two years old, and you need a husband."

"What I need is a good lawyer and an understanding judge so I can get back to work," Darcy commented.

"What I need is lunch," Bob moaned.

"Men . . . they're such babies," Darcy taunted.

Betty handed Bob a stack of plates and turned to Darcy. "Why don't you two get out of here so we can finish up. You know where I keep the silverware and the napkins."

And Darcy knew exactly where they were because if there was one thing she remembered about life in Greenhaven . . . nothing ever changed. Day after day, year after year, it was the same old boring routine. But Darcy had escaped.

"PASS THE PEAS, please."

"Where's the salt?"

"You don't need any more salt. It isn't good for you."

"Is the tea sweetened?"

"Are there any drumsticks left?"

Darcy smiled at the chaos that always seemed to occur during mealtimes in the Carson household. With Bob and Sue's four children and Steve and Janice's two, the conversation was lively and the food disappeared quickly. She loved her nieces and nephews, but it was times like these that she was glad they weren't her kids.

After the leftovers were packed away and the dishes washed, Bob, Steve and their families left to go to their own homes only a couple of miles away from their parents' farm. Darcy and her mother sat on the front porch, enjoying the crisp autumn afternoon while her father, J.W., snoozed in a recliner in the den, oblivious to the football game on television.

"I never really appreciate quiet until the children leave," Betty admitted. Abruptly, she lifted her gaze from her knitting. "Not that I don't love having the grandkids come over. Children are the greatest joy in this world."

"Mother..." Darcy warned.

"I know. Subtlety." Her mother laughed. "But you can't blame me for trying. I just don't want you to miss out on anything."

"I'm not. Honestly, I couldn't be happier."

Betty rocked back and forth while her fingers automatically maneuvered the needles through a series of intricate stitches. "Don't you miss anything here?"

Darcy reached across the narrow space between her chair and her mother's and rested her hand on Betty's arm. She looked at her mother with great affection as she spoke. "I miss you and Dad very much."

Betty patted her daughter's hand and smiled. "I know you do, dear. But I meant the farm, the animals, the peace and quiet..." She gestured in an all-encompassing sweep of the area. "I thought you enjoyed growing up here."

Darcy let her gaze drift off the wide, covered porch over the well-tended flower beds that surrounded the yard. A few hardy yellow chrysanthemums still provided cheerful color against the rich, dark earth. Whitewashed fences marked off rectangular corrals around the large barn. A sweet-faced Jersey cow dozed, sharing the shade of the barn with a fat Welsh pony that J.W. kept around for the grandkids. And behind the barn, as far as she could see, were gently rolling hills, covered with the drying stubble of that season's corn crop.

It was all so familiar, and yet so alien. After twelve years of living in some of the largest cities in the world, Darcy was used to the sun being blocked by tall buildings rather than ancient, heavy-limbed trees. The only animals she saw were dispirited carriage horses, crisply outfitted police mounts, stray cats who haunted the alleys and pampered dogs leading their owners on walks.

And the sounds. How could she compare the screech of traffic, the blasts of music from passing cars, the constant murmur of voices to the melodies of birds, the whisper of the wind through the leaves or the click of her mother's knitting needles? It was funny, but she didn't notice the absence of any of those things while she was in the city. But here, wrapped in a gentleness that was almost palpable, she realized there were elements she missed.

"It's nice to be back," she admitted, but hastily added when she saw her mother's eyes brighten, "for a visit."

"There's still no special man back in Los Angeles?"

Darcy shook her head. "No. I've been too busy." She didn't mention the reporter she'd met while in Riyadh when she was covering the Gulf war. He'd had everything she wanted in a man—sophistication, education, ambition—and he had looked almost as good in person as he did on camera. But with the abrupt ending of the war, he'd moved on to a new assignment in Tokyo, leaving her only a brief farewell note.

"Then I don't suppose you'd mind spending a little time with Nellie's son, would you? He's been so lonely since his wife died." Betty focused her attention on her knitting in an obvious move to avoid meeting her daughter's disapproving gaze. "I didn't actually meet his wife," Betty continued. "She died before he bought the Willowby place. Such a shame. Those kids were so little. Even if they are boys, they need a mother. Poor Nellie tries, but she can't keep up with—"

"No." Darcy's voice was low, and her tone was firm. "I'm not interested in *spending time* with a man who raises turkeys and kids. Weren't you listening to our conversation in the kitchen? That combination is not my idea of a dream come true."

"Now Darcy. He's a nice man...hardworking, sober, a real homebody. He's the type who'd always be home for dinner. You wouldn't have to worry about him hanging out in bars and chasing women."

Darcy made no attempt to hide a groan. The man had none of the qualities she was looking for in a mate. In fact, he sounded downright boring. "No...

no . . . no. I don't care if he'd be home for dinner, because I don't want to have to be there to cook it. It would probably be me hanging out in the bar."

"Darcy!" Her mother's expression was horrified. "You go to bars?"

"Only when the nightclubs are closed."

"Darcy!" Betty repeated more loudly as she clutched her hands to her chest, her knitting wadded into a ball.

"I'm joking, Mother." Darcy's clear blue eyes twinkled.

Slowly, Betty's hands relaxed as she considered her daughter's denial.

"Anyway, I'm not going to be here long enough to meet this guy. I expect a phone call from Charlie, my agent, tomorrow or the next day. He's trying to find me a good lawyer who can work out some sort of deal."

"Does that mean you're admitting you did something wrong?"

"No, it means that I don't want to go through a lengthy trial. That's not the sort of publicity I need."

The needles began tapping rhythmically again. "Well, it wouldn't hurt for you to take a little time off. I'll bet the people who watch that channel will miss you. If your station gets enough letters maybe they'll give you a raise."

Darcy threaded her fingers through her auburn hair, pushing it away from her face. "That's not how it works. When reporters are out of sight, they're out of mind. If I stay off the air for a month, I might as well look for a new station.''

''Don't be silly. Your audience can't help but miss you.''

Pride was evident in Betty's voice, but Darcy knew it was more a protective motherly-sort-of defensive gesture rather than because Betty was pleased with her daughter's career. It wasn't that Betty didn't approve of Darcy's success in television; Betty simply wasn't impressed by it.

''Well, I'm not going to worry about being forgotten until I talk to my agent,'' Darcy declared positively.

''Since you probably won't be here long, you won't mind if I call Nell and see if her son would like to meet you.''

''Mother...'' Darcy warned.

Betty shrugged. ''He'll probably be busy anyway.''

''I'm sure there's lots of things he has to do at his turkey ranch...or whatever it is you'd call a place that raises turkeys.''

''I think it would be called a turkey farm,'' Betty commented.

''That makes it sound like he plants little turkey seeds in the ground like Dad plants corn.''

''Well, regardless of what it's called, it's a good, honest way to making a living.''

''I didn't say it isn't,'' Darcy protested. ''It's just not the sort of life I'm interested in.''

''You never know,'' Betty said mysteriously. ''Remember what the preacher said this morning... *God works in mysterious ways.*''

Darcy shook her head. "Maybe so. But surely God wouldn't play such an awful trick on me."

"Darcy, you're blaspheming again."

"Mother, you're meddling again."

"That's what mothers are for."

Darcy stood up and stretched. "I'm going to go inside and catch the local news. It pays to keep up with my competition. Who knows when some sweet young thing from Des Moines will make that giant leap to L.A.?"

"Just like you did," Betty reminded Darcy with an annoying perception.

"Yes, just like I did." A fresh wave of anxiety pulsed through her at the reminder of how easy it would be for someone to step into her network shoes.

Betty watched her daughter walk into the house. She waited until she heard Darcy and J.W.'s voices mixed with the opening music of the evening news program. Betty set aside her knitting, being careful to anchor the needles so none of the stitches would slide off. She reached into her apron pocket and took out the receiver of the cordless telephone Darcy had given her parents for Christmas last year.

There was a calm, optimistic smile on Betty's face as she extended the antenna, then dialed a number.

"Hello, Nellie," she said. "What did you think of my daughter?" She paused as she listened to Nell's response. "Yes, I think she's beautiful, too. But then I might be a little prejudiced."

Betty glanced around, carefully checking to see if anyone was within hearing distance before she continued.

"Nell, the reason I'm calling is that I think your son and my daughter would make a perfect couple. Now how can we get them together . . . ?"

# Chapter Two

"No! Absolutely not. I have no interest in meeting a stuck-up snoop from Los Angeles."

Luke flipped a pancake over in the skillet, then poured milk into three glasses on the breakfast table. Lifting the golden brown pancake out, he added it to a heaping stack before carrying them to the table, too.

He stepped into the kitchen doorway and called up the stairs, "Greg, Adam, Scott...come eat." Turning back to his mother who was packing lunches, two into paper sacks and one into a Bugs Bunny lunch box, he continued their conversation as if there had been no disruption. "And I don't need my mother to set me up with women."

"But Luke, I'm just trying to help," Nell explained as she folded the tops of the bags and wrote the two older boys' names on them with a magic marker. "You're too young to spend so much time alone."

"Alone!" he exclaimed, one corner of his mouth lifting in a grin. "With three sons and my mother sharing my house and fifty thousand turkeys living in my yard, I'm *never* alone."

Nell heaved an exaggerated sigh. "You know what I mean."

"Are you trying to kick me out of the nest?"

Nell glanced around her. "Don't be silly. This is your nest. If anyone's going to leave, it's me."

"Ah ha! So now we're getting to the truth of the matter. You're trying to escape this quiet little household," Luke teased as he poured himself a cup of coffee.

The thunder of Nike-shod feet on wooden stairs drowned out her denial. The two younger boys reached the doorway to the kitchen at the same time and wedged through the opening with a great deal of pushing and shoving.

"Boys, settle down!" Luke demanded in a low, calm voice that immediately separated his sons and brought them quietly to their chairs. "Adam, get your snake off the table. You know how your grandmother feels about him."

"His snake ate my gum," Scott complained.

"Snakes don't eat gum," Luke pointed out.

"Then Adam took it," Scott declared indignantly.

"Now that I can believe," Luke agreed. "Adam, leave your brother's things alone."

"Why can't I have a pet?" With obvious envy, Scott eyed the garter snake's striped head as it poked out of Adam's T-shirt pocket. "Greg has a cat, and Adam has a snake *and* a gerbil." Scott's lower lip quivered dramatically. "I haven't ever had a pet."

"Maybe for your seventh birthday," Luke answered with paternal caution.

"But..."

"Eat your breakfast or you're going to miss the school bus." Luke sat down and helped himself to several fluffy pancakes. "Adam, did you finish your homework last night?"

"Didn't have any," Adam answered with his mouth full, which earned him a reprimanding look from both his grandmother and his father.

"I hope you're not letting it slide. I don't want to see any F's on your report card."

"I'm doing okay," Adam insisted.

Moving at a more leisurely pace, Greg entered the room and sat at his place . "I've got driver's ed. today, Dad," he said as he loaded his plate.

"Can Dave's father bring you home?" Luke asked. "I'm going to be loading turkeys all day and your grandma will be in Council Bluffs."

"I'll ask, but I'm sure he will." Greg wiped up the syrup on his plate with his last bite of pancake.

The honk of a horn brought a renewed burst of noise and confusion as all three boys leapt to their feet, raced to the stairs where they had left their books and coats, then returned to the kitchen to grab their lunches. They called their goodbyes as they ran out the door and down the driveway to where the school bus waited.

Luke shut the door and shook his head as he returned to the table to finish his breakfast. His mother sat across from him, nibbling at a slice of whole wheat toast.

"I can't understand why you'd want to leave such a calm, pleasant place as this," he joked, once again resuming their conversation. "You'd be so lonely without me and the boys."

"Sure, I'd miss you guys." Nell gave him an unapologetic look. "But I wouldn't mind living alone for a while."

"Now I'm getting a complex." Luke's smile faded as he studied his mother's serious expression. His wife and his father had died within a couple months of each other so it had been a natural step for his mother to move in with Luke's family. Until this moment, it had never occurred to him that she might want to live somewhere else. "You really mean that, don't you?"

Nell reached for Luke's empty plate, but his hand on hers stopped her. It was obvious she wanted to avoid hurting his feelings. But it was equally apparent that this subject had been on her mind for some time.

"Mom, you know you're always welcome here," he spoke to fill the silence of her hesitation. "But if you'd prefer getting a place of your own, I'll understand."

Nell's smile was wistful and tinged with maternal sacrifice. "I wouldn't leave until you and the boys have someone to take care of you."

Luke shook his head. "I don't need a wife. I can handle things around here."

"No you can't," she stated positively. "It takes a lot of work to run this farm. And keeping up with the boys is a full-time job."

"Then I'll hire someone," he replied with a shrug. "Paying someone to take care of the kids and the house would be simpler than getting married again."

"But it wouldn't hurt for you to be open-minded about remarriage. You never know when the perfect woman might stumble into your life. If you were to start dating again . . ."

"I *have* dated."

"Taking the secretary at the farmers' co-op out to lunch or having that woman at the feed store deliver your feed and stay for a cup of coffee don't count as dates. Maybe if you called Betty's daughter, Darcy, the two of you could go out for dinner and a movie."

"Ah ha!" he exclaimed, a knowing twinkle leaping into his gray eyes. "So that's what this is all about."

"It wouldn't hurt you to be nice to her. She's not going to be here long, so it's not like there's any risk that either of you will get too serious." Nell finished cleaning the table and opened the dishwasher. "Consider it a sort of practice run."

Luke opened his mouth to protest, but the ring of the telephone interrupted. His mother answered it, then held out the receiver to him.

"It's Adam's principal. *Again,*" she added pointedly. "He says Adam brought his snake to school and was chasing girls around the playground, scaring them with it."

Luke pushed his chair back, walked to the wall phone and took the receiver with a sigh. He talked with Adam's principal and teachers more often than he liked. If there was any mischief going on, Adam was always the one to be involved.

"Yes, this is Luke Calloway." He listened while Mr. Birch, the junior-high principal, repeated the details of the incident. "No sir, I didn't know he took the snake to school with him. He was running late, so I'm sure it was just an oversight." Luke rolled his eyes as

Mr. Birch continued to rant about the inappropriateness of carrying a snake in one's pocket and using it to frighten other children. "Yes. I'll come pick it up right away. And yes, I'll speak to Adam about it this evening."

He hung up the phone and turned to face his mother. "You wouldn't be able to go to the school, would you?" he asked hopefully.

"No, I'm afraid not. I'm supposed to be at the church in fifteen minutes. It's our day to feed the homeless."

He glanced at the kitchen clock. "Damn...er... darn, I need to get those turkeys loaded. I was hoping to get in three trips today."

His mother was doing nothing to hide her "I told you so" expression.

Luke took his worn baseball cap off the row of hooks near the back door and jammed it on his head. "Okay, Mom. You win this round. I'll call Dorothy..."

"Darcy," his mother corrected.

"...whoever...I'll call her this evening." He turned to his mother and promised, "But nothing's going to come of this. It'll be one night and that's all."

Nell's smile was pure innocence. "God works in mysterious ways."

"Not even God could make this relationship work," Luke muttered as he stalked out of the kitchen.

"SHE SAID NO."

Nell looked up from her cross-stitching. "What on earth did you say to her?"

"You make it sound as if it's *my* fault." Luke walked into the living room and plopped on the couch. After a brief, *very* brief, conversation with Darcy Carson, his feelings were an odd mixture of relief and annoyance. He wiped his wet palms against his jeans and cursed the sudden attack of nerves he'd had while calling the woman. The last time he'd asked someone for a date, he'd been a teenager. And it was a discomfort that had worsened with age. "I was polite and to the point."

His mother threw up her hands. "I can just imagine." She mimicked in a deep voice, *"Dorothy... er... Darcy, you wouldn't want to go out on a date with me, would you?"*

"I didn't say that," he denied indignantly.

"Then why wouldn't she go out with you? You're an attractive, eligible man and she's a beautiful, single woman. How dare she turn down your invitation!"

Luke picked up the newspaper. "It's no big deal, Mom. She said she was expecting a call tomorrow and didn't plan on being here this weekend." He didn't add that she hadn't sounded any more enthusiastic about the idea of a blind date than he was. She'd been friendly, but definitely distant.

"I don't see why both of you are being so hardheaded," his mother murmured, her disappointment obvious.

"It just wasn't meant to be." Luke opened the newspaper and tried to focus his thoughts on the page in front of him. But soon his eyelids began to droop. It had been a hard day. The trip to the school had thrown him off schedule, so when he returned from his third trip to the processor with a load of turkeys, the rest of the family was just sitting down to dinner. After the meal, he'd worked with the boys on their homework, had an obligatory talk with Adam about his pets, then supervised their baths and bedtime. When he would have preferred collapsing on the couch and catching the end of "Monday Night Football," his mother had prompted him to make the dreaded call.

Being shot down before he could even get the entire question out of his mouth had been the perfect ending to a normal, imperfect day.

"DARCY, THERE'S SOMEONE on the phone for you," Betty called up the stairs. "I think it might be your agent."

"I'll take it in your bedroom," Darcy shouted as she hurried from her room down the hall to her parents' room. She sat stiffly on the edge of the bed and picked up the receiver. Hopefully it would be the call she'd been expecting for the last three days. She'd been as jumpy as a frog on a hot sidewalk, holding her breath every time the phone rang. "I've got it, Mother." She waited for the click, then answered.

"Hello Darcy. How's it going in the heartland of America? Have you milked any cows lately?"

"Very funny, Charlie." Her sense of humor had been missing in action ever since she left California last week. Her case so dominated her thoughts that even her mother had stopped trying to make conversation. "So tell me what's going on in the heart*less-*

land of America...are they willing to drop the charges?''

There was a moment of eloquent silence before Charlie responded. "Well, not exactly."

"What does that mean?"

"The charges still stand against you, but they've offered Larry immunity if he cooperates with the prosecution."

Darcy gasped. "Larry! He wouldn't..." Larry was a long-time contact who had often helped her uncover difficult stories.

"Yes, he would," Charlie confirmed. "It's amazing what the threat of a grand jury investigation will do."

"The grand jury?" The words escaped in a pained sigh. The room began spinning around, and Darcy squeezed her eyes tightly shut as her fingers dug into the antique quilt. Oddly, one part of her conscious mind focused on the intricate patterns of the scraps of material beneath her hand, scraps her great-grandmother had lovingly stitched together during her first long, cold winter as a bride.

But the other part of her mind was scrambling to refocus after the devastating news that there would be a grand jury investigation. "I thought you said we should be able to make some sort of deal with the lab?"

"We tried. But apparently, they're tired of the negative publicity, and they're willing to fight this one all the way to the end."

Darcy pushed back on the bed so her shoulders were braced against the headboard. She honestly hadn't believed things would go so far. No one had been hurt . . . not physically, at least. Perhaps the blow to Purity Products' pocketbook had been an even more painful wound.

"The good news is that we've hired the best defense attorney in southern California," Charlie added. "His name is Sheldon Kramer."

"I've heard of him. He's got a reputation for being tough and creative, which is exactly what I need."

"He's already pushing things along. If the grand jury passes down an indictment, the trial will be sometime in early December."

"That's awfully quick, isn't it?" Darcy was well aware of how backed up the court system was in L.A., and the speedy scheduling added to her surprise.

"Yes it is. But the media is still gnawing on this like a pit bull on a soup bone, and I think the prosecution would like to push this case through as quickly as possible. They've even asked for a change of venue should the case go to trial. They're afraid that all the animal rights activists and ecologists in the area will raise a stink, not to mention the outcry from your audience. They really miss you here."

Darcy managed a small smile. It was comforting to know that her reputation wasn't totally ruined. "I can be back in L.A. by Saturday—"

"No, I don't think that's a good idea," Charlie interrupted. "Things are still too hot here, and the media will be camping on your doorstep. I think it's better that you lie low until your court date. The grand jury will want to talk to you next week, but you can fly in and fly out quietly with as little fanfare as possible.

We don't want the prosecution to be able to say you're trying to milk the situation for publicity. We're playing up the angle that you were innocently swept into the incident and were just reporting what was happening."

"That *is* what really happened," Darcy commented hopefully.

Another long pause was followed by Charlie clearing his throat unencouragingly. "It would help if they didn't have those tape recordings."

Darcy frowned as she tried to think of what he could possibly be talking about. "What tape recordings? I don't remember..."

"It seems that Larry recorded some of his telephone conversations with you."

"That's illegal!" she gasped.

"Yes, and it's also very damaging to your claim of having no prior knowledge of the break-in. I haven't heard the tapes, but the rumor is that there's a lengthy discussion of how you wished Earthhope would hit Purity's lab during sweeps week so you could get the story. I think you even made the comment that perhaps they could be encouraged to stage something dramatic."

"I was just running off at the mouth. I *didn't* set it up," Darcy protested frantically. "They already had it planned. I only followed up on the tip of the time and place."

"I know that and you know that. But there are a lot of people saying that isn't the way it happened."

Darcy rubbed her trembling fingers across her forehead. "Oh God," she breathed, not in sacrilege, but in a desperate plea for heavenly help.

"Look, you need to relax and collect your thoughts," Charlie continued. "Sheldon will call and let you know exactly when the grand jury will want to see you. But until then, try not to worry too much. We're doing all we can."

"How about the station?" Darcy asked, her voice uncharacteristically weak.

"They're still behind you, but they've made it very clear that your leave of absence will continue until the case is settled. So you stay put in the bosom of your family until we're ready for you here."

For several minutes after she hung up the phone, Darcy stayed on the bed. Her muscles didn't have the capability of movement and even the simple act of breathing was difficult. Possibilities and probabilities flashed through her brain. Usually so logical, right now she couldn't manage to curb the panic that gripped her mind, dulling her senses.

Her career was her whole life. She had known all along that the situation was serious. But she'd never considered, even for an instant, that the case would go to court. As an investigative reporter she'd had several unhappy subjects threaten lawsuits. But no one had ever followed through. Darcy had always been careful, even when she had tiptoed on the edge of other legal, moral and ethical issues.

It hurt that Larry had betrayed her. She'd trusted him, perhaps in hindsight, too much. She wished she could remember what they'd discussed on the telephone because she knew how easily joking banter could be misinterpreted when taken out of context.

She pushed back the veil of auburn hair that had fallen across her face. How would she survive the next three and a half weeks? Her fate was in unknown hands, and she had absolutely no control over the outcome. For a woman who was accustomed to charging forward and making her own luck, this helplessness was a shattering experience.

Of course, her parents would be delighted that her stay would be extended. And Darcy knew she would have to make more of an effort not to let her worries make her such an unbearable recluse. Her mother had been after her to be friendly and to get out more. Maybe she should have accepted that guy's—what was his name?—offer of dinner. But, at the time, she'd thought she would be back in L.A. and it didn't seem sensible to make plans for the weekend.

Darcy shrugged. Actually, she wasn't too sorry. She wasn't interested in spending time with a farmer, especially a widower with three kids. They would have nothing in common other than their Iowa roots, but she'd left all that behind long ago. Besides, she doubted she'd be very good company right now anyway.

# Chapter Three

"I can't believe it! It's almost four o'clock." Betty rushed around the kitchen, uncharacteristically flustered.

Darcy poured a glass of orange juice and leaned against the refrigerator. She knew without being told that it must be time for the county fair. It was the only time of year that her mother acted like a normal, insecure person.

"These pies have to be there by five o'clock. The judging will be at six." Betty carefully removed one of her secret recipe apple pies from the oven and set it on a cooling rack, then returned to the oven for a perfectly latticed cherry pie. As soon as both pies were safely settled, Betty threw up her hands and continued in a frantic tone. "J.W. is still in the field grinding silage . . . I've still got to finish the cakes . . . they don't have to be there until seven . . . I just don't know how I'm going to get these pies to the fair."

"Calm down, Mother. I can take them."

"No, you can't. Then I wouldn't have a car to take my cakes later."

"I'll drop off the pies..." At her mother's stricken look, Darcy amended, "I'll carefully *deliver* the pies, then I'll hurry back here and pick up you and your cakes."

Betty paused in mid-stride between the sink and the table. "I know... I'll bet Nell's sending her pies, too. Maybe she'll be able to stop by and pick up mine on her way." She crossed to the phone. "I'll give her a call."

Darcy assumed her part in the scenario was over, so she strolled into the living room and turned on the television, tuning in to her favorite soap opera. Occasionally her assignments had stuck her in out-of-the-way towns where she would turn on the television more for company than entertainment. Even with several months between these soapy sessions, Darcy picked up on the story lines with no difficulty.

She wished she'd driven her car here or rented one. Her dad usually had his truck out on the farm somewhere, and her mother needed the family car. Darcy was getting a little stir-crazy, having been tied to the farm, leaving only to accompany her mother to church or bridge club meetings or to meet old friends. But the few times she'd had lunch with her friends, they'd been inconvenienced by having to drive out to pick her up and then bring her back to the farm. When she flew back to L.A. for the grand jury depositions, she decided she would drive her car back. It would take three days, two if she pushed it, but after all, she wasn't in a big rush. There was nothing happening in Greenhaven that she couldn't afford to miss.

"Darcy, we've got it all worked out." Betty rushed into the living room, a note of relief in her voice. She slid to a halt and stared at Darcy. "You're not going to wear that, are you?"

Darcy looked down at her comfortable velour sweatsuit. "What's wrong with this?"

"Oh nothing. It's just not quite appropriate for the fair."

Perhaps her wits were getting dull from her lack of activity, but Darcy was having trouble keeping up with the conversation. "I didn't think you needed me to go to the fair."

"Of course I need you. Do you think I'd trust Nellie's son with my prizewinning pies?"

The fog was beginning to clear. "So I'm riding to the fair with that man you haven't stopped talking about all week?"

"Yes, and he'll be here in ten minutes. Now hurry upstairs and change clothes. There's no telling who you'll run into. You wouldn't want your old classmates to see you like that, would you?"

Darcy sensed it was hopeless to argue, but her background in journalism required some sort of debate. "I'm sure Nell's son can handle transporting your pies. I'll stay and help you with your cakes."

Her mother's expression changed to one of desperation. "But you *have* to go. I know I can trust you to take care of my pies. If you have them, I won't worry, and I can concentrate on my cakes. I need just one more win to make the Mills County Apple Pie Hall of Fame."

The sound of a truck stopping outside and the slamming of a door generated a renewed plea. "Please Darcy. Do this for me."

Darcy stood and gave her mother a suspicious look. "You and Nell wouldn't have cooked this up to get me and her son together, would you?"

Betty's eyes widened innocently. "Darcy, would I endanger my chances in the pie contest for something like that?"

"You're answering my question with a question, Mother. I smell a setup."

The sound of the doorbell echoed through the living room and Betty leapt forward. With a none too gentle shove toward the stairs, she avoided a response. Instead she said, "Now hurry up. I'll let Luke in, then pack the pies. We'll talk about this later."

"Yes, we will," Darcy promised, but another push propelled her up the first two steps. Resisting the urge to lean over the landing rail to get a glimpse of her driver-to-be, she went directly to her bedroom. Since the man had already called her once, Darcy suspected he'd had some part in the scheme. Poor man, he was probably desperate to get away from all those kids and turkeys. Just a homely farmer anxious for a night on the town.

Darcy dressed quickly, not taking particular care with her appearance. But after being in the limelight for so many years, her sense of style was as much a part of her as her baby-blue eyes. Fifteen minutes later, she walked back down the stairs dressed in tight, fashionably faded jeans, a sequined cowboy shirt and boots.

"There she is," Betty announced with a great deal more enthusiasm than the moment deserved. "Darcy dear, come meet Luke Calloway. Luke, this is my daughter, Darcy."

Darcy's level gaze landed somewhere in the middle of a broad chest, then moved upward over a firm, square chin, a full, sensual mouth and a strong, straight nose to skid to a halt at a pair of cool gray eyes. At that instant, she was positive that this man was no more excited at the prospect of spending the evening with her than she was with him. The realization left her curiously shaken . . . and with a firm resolve to get this over with as quickly as possible.

"Nice to meet you," she said, giving him one of her practiced smiles.

"You, too," he answered with a matching lack of sincerity.

Betty glanced from one to the other, then hurried back to the kitchen. "Come on, kids. You need to get going so you won't be late." She handed them each a cardboard carton with a pie tucked inside, then led the way to the front door. "Now don't hurry back. J.W. and I will be along as soon as he gets back and I finish the cakes."

Luke held the door with his free hand while Darcy left the pie on the coffee table long enough to pull on her leather jacket and slip the strap of her purse over her shoulder. After picking up the box, she stepped through the doorway and almost froze in her tracks as she looked at the vehicle in front of her.

The decades had not been kind to the pickup truck. At least one dent for every one of its dozen or more years scarred its sides. A thick layer of dust completely obscured the color of its paint and only a more recently added giant wishbone surrounded with the words Wishbone Acres was visible through the grime.

Sucking in a deep breath, Darcy gave her mother a last, unforgiving look, then scooted onto the blanket that covered the seat in the truck's cab. Luke added his box to the one Darcy held on her lap. Two more were stacked on the seat next to her, blessedly providing a solid division between her and the tall, silent man who walked to the driver's side and slid behind the steering wheel.

The engine sputtered to life and the gears growled into place. As they drove down the driveway Darcy tried to ignore the swirl of white turkey feathers that boiled out of the back of the truck. Defying the laws of gravity and all sense of good taste, most of the feathers formed a mini-tornado in the truck's bed with only a few escaping to flutter along behind.

If the seat had ever had springs, they had long ago died, leaving Darcy's behind bumping on the floorboard when the vehicle bounced across the cattle guard at the end of the drive. Country and western music blared from the radio, and Darcy suspected its volume was to discourage any small talk between the two occupants.

She sneaked another glance at him, wondering what thoughts were hidden behind those expressionless gray eyes. Thick dark brown hair was combed back from a side part, but an appealing lock managed to fall across one corner of his forehead, making him look younger than she'd imagined. Only the occasional flexing of the muscle along the curve of his square jaw revealed he was not as calm as he appeared.

Darcy didn't know why she had automatically guessed he'd be balding and either too tall and lanky or too short and paunchy. Having grown up with farmers and ranchers, it had been unfair and unjustified of her to assume he'd be unattractive. There were as many good-looking men in Iowa as there were anywhere else, with the possible exception of Hollywood. But Hollywood could hardly be called a typical cross section of the population.

Actually, she would have preferred the plainness she'd expected. Somehow, it would be easier to get through the evening if he wasn't so darn handsome.

Firmly holding the boxes so they didn't jostle, Darcy hoped her mother was satisfied. If Darcy lived through the evening, she vowed to tell Betty exactly what she thought about being manipulated and forced into such an uncomfortable situation.

Betty watched until the truck disappeared down the county road, then she picked up the telephone receiver and dialed a number.

"Hello, Nellie. It worked. They're on their way."

AFTER SEVERAL MILES of silence, Darcy began to view the trip as a challenge. She'd faced tough interviews before and been able to draw them out. By the end of the conversation, even the most distant people had warmed to her natural, but well-trained, friendliness.

"Mother said you have three sons," she said, speaking loudly to be heard over the music. "Are they going to the fair this evening?"

Without taking his eyes off the road, he answered, "They're coming with my mother later."

"I saw them last Sunday in church. They're all very nice-looking boys, especially the little one. I can tell he's a sweetheart."

The straight line of Luke's mouth softened and the fan of lines at the corner of his eyes deepened as an unconscious smile sneaked through his defenses.

"That's Scott," Luke replied. "And yes, he's a real charmer. But all my boys are pretty good kids." Fatherly pride obviously overcame his displeasure with the current situation.

"I didn't see you at the service."

"I was there, but I had to leave early because I had an emergency at the farm."

Even though any emergency was serious, there was something about his answer that struck her as funny. "You had a *turkey* emergency?" She immediately regretted the question because she knew it sounded flippant.

But instead of a reproachful look, there was a tiny glint of humor in his eyes when he glanced toward her. Darcy was unreasonably pleased to discover that, even though he was trying hard not to show it, there was a sense of humor beneath that bland expression.

"Yes, as a matter of fact, there are turkey emergencies," he commented dryly. "At this time of year when two-thirds of my birds are ready to be marketed, almost anything can create a crisis."

Since Darcy knew next to nothing about turkeys, she couldn't think of any intelligent questions to ask. When Luke's attention returned to the road, she sighed and gave up on trying to make conversation. The fairgrounds were only a few miles away, and there was no reason she and Luke would have to stay together once they arrived.

He steered into the parking area that was really nothing more than a smooth, packed-down field and parked the truck. But just as Darcy was preparing herself to tell this man a permanent "goodbye," he turned off the engine and shifted to face her again.

"I don't suppose we ever had a chance, did we?" he remarked, an appealing half smile lifting one corner of his mouth.

Darcy didn't know how to respond. Instead of feeling relief that he was going to let her go without an argument, Darcy was disappointed. There could never be anything long-term about their relationship, but it might have been fun to have an attractive man make the time pass more quickly.

"Once our mothers were determined to get us together, we might as well have given in right then," he continued. "Look, I'm sorry. There are probably a hundred things you'd rather be doing this evening, and a hundred other people you'd rather be doing them with. I admit I wasn't too thrilled with the idea of a blind date, especially one set up by my mother."

"I know what you mean."

"Dammit, I'm thirty-six years old. I don't need my mother's help with women." His expression softened. "But I didn't have to take it out on you. We didn't start out well, and I'll take full blame. Now that we're here, why don't we make the best of things? If I remember correctly, county fairs can be a whole lot of fun.'' The smile spread like quicksilver to his eyes.

It was easy to see where little Scott got his charm. Once this man set his mind to it, Darcy could easily imagine that he would be irresistible. However, considering her temporary circumstances, she felt safe enough to accept his olive branch of peace.

"Sure, why not," she answered. "I never missed a fair when I was a kid. But it's been years . . . Lord, I hate to think how many . . . since I've been to one."

"Great!" Luke seemed genuinely pleased. "There's just one thing you have to promise."

"Sure. What?" Darcy had no idea what he had in mind, but the twinkle in his eyes led her to blindly agree.

"You have to promise that if the evening does go well, no matter how much fun we have or how well we get along, you will *not* tell your mother. And I won't tell mine. We wouldn't want to encourage them."

Darcy held out her hand. "Agreed. Mothers who are frustrated matchmakers can be very dangerous."

He chuckled, a deep, rich sound that warmed the interior of the truck's cab much better than the rustic heater had. He reached out and took her hand, intending to shake it. But the electricity that pulsed from his fingers to hers and back again left him with a dazed look on his face that Darcy was certain must match her own.

"Uh...we'd better get these pies in...right away." He jerked his hand away more abruptly than necessary, almost knocking the boxes holding his mother's baked goods onto the floor.

Darcy didn't wait for him to run around and open her door, but yanked on the handle and pushed.

"It's a little tricky," Luke commented. "I'll get it."

"No, that's okay." She shoved her shoulder against the door and was pleased that it opened with an ear-splitting squawk. "I know what Santa can bring you for Christmas," she remarked as she carefully eased out, her arms cradling the two boxes.

"A new car?"

She chuckled. "I don't think that would fit in his sleigh. I was thinking more along the lines of a case of WD-40."

He looked from her to the truck, then back at her. His mouth opened as if he was about to say something, but then snapped shut.

"Should I lock my door?" she asked.

"Are you kidding? I could leave the keys in the ignition and a hundred-dollar bill in the glove box, and still couldn't get anyone to take it off my hands." His hands were full, so he kicked the door shut, then walked around to join Darcy. "Do you know where we're supposed to take these pies?"

"They used to judge them in the home economics building. Unless they've moved it, I think I can find it."

Darcy's memory proved accurate and they were able to deliver the pies before the entry deadline. After filling out the forms and sticking a numbered plastic stick, red for the cherry and green for the apple, into the middle of the pastries, she found empty spots for them on the overcrowded tables, then turned to leave.

Luke was waiting for her at the door. "Are you hungry? Or would you rather look at the animals first?"

"It doesn't matter to me."

"Okay, then let's hit the barns now. We can eat after the judging."

They headed toward the triple rows of long, low metallic buildings at the edge of the fairgrounds. Darcy wasn't the least surprised when they entered the poultry shed first.

"Let me guess," she teased, "we're going to look at the turkeys, right?"

"Well...I have a vested interest," he admitted. "My two youngest boys have entries through 4-H. I want to see how the judging went today." They passed dozens of stacked cages, each providing a temporary home for one or two chickens. Some of the breeds Darcy recognized, but there were many strange, exotic birds that barely resembled chickens.

"There they are," Luke announced, pointing to a block of four cages, all adorned with ribbons.

The wire enclosures were much larger than those holding the chickens, but still the turkeys looked crowded and uncomfortable. "They can barely move around in there," she said sympathetically. "I'll bet they can't wait to get home."

"I doubt that. They're going to be on someone's dinner table soon."

Darcy tried not to react negatively, but he must have sensed her distaste.

"That's what turkeys are raised for, you know," he added matter-of-factly.

"I know. And I don't mind it when they're running loose until . . . well, until their moment of truth." She ran her fingertips over the large red, white and blue grand champion ribbon that adorned one of the cages. "It's just that I hate cages."

Luke nodded. "Yes, I know what you mean. I never cage my birds unless they're here or on their way to market."

"That's what got me into trouble," Darcy continued thoughtfully. "I was involved in a sort of protest."

"A protest against turkeys?"

"No, against animals being used for nonmedical tests or being tortured unnecessarily."

"But why would that get you into trouble? I thought California was so socially aware. Don't they allow protests?"

"Protests, yes. Riots, no." Darcy could hear the nervous ring in her short, mirthless laugh. "I think Earthhope had planned to break in and release the animals all along. I guess I even sort of expected it, in the back of my mind. But since I was aware of the planning of the protests, and approved of it both because of the animals and because I was looking for an exciting human interest story, the lab believes I knew about the planned destruction and could have stopped it."

"So they filed charges against you?"

"Yes, because I'm the most visible target. It wouldn't look good for them to prosecute Earthhope. But a nosy reporter makes a very public sacrificial lamb."

Luke was looking at her curiously as if weighing her story. "But you think you'll beat the charges, don't you?"

Darcy dragged her fingers through her hair. "God, I hope so. It took me years to get where I am. Ever since I was old enough to recognize the difference between good and bad reporting, being a newscaster was all I've ever wanted to be. I don't know what I'd do if I suddenly lost it all. How does a person start over when they're thirty-two years old?"

"I did." His voice was low and dark with emotion.

Darcy's gaze was drawn to his face. "You did? Why?"

"I was thirty-two years old when my wife died. I was left with three small boys, a big house filled with memories and a job I hated. So I quit my job, sold everything and bought the farm down the road from your parents'."

"Just like that?"

"Just like that."

"What sort of job did you have?"

He chuckled, obviously anticipating her response. "I was a dentist."

She didn't try to mask her surprise. "And you gave it all up for a farm?" At his confirming nod, she added, "But why turkeys?"

"Because they don't have teeth!"

"Luke!" she scolded. But even as she tried to keep the conversation serious, she couldn't help but notice there was an intriguing flash of green in the misty depths of his eyes.

"Okay, that wasn't the main reason," he admitted. "My grandfather raised turkeys. He did pretty well, too, and that was before turkey meat became a sort of health food. Eventually, though, he sold the place when a developer decided Gramps' turkey farm was the ideal location for a shopping mall."

"But it was such a drastic change in your life-style."

"Yes, it was. And it's not one I would have had the guts to try if my world hadn't fallen apart." His look was understanding, but not sympathetic. "Maybe you should have a backup plan...just in case."

## Chapter Four

"Dad, did you see my ribbon? Well, it isn't exactly *my* ribbon. But my turkey won it, so that sort of makes it mine, doesn't it?"

"Yes, I saw it, Scotty." Luke smiled as he looked down at his youngest son. He, of all Luke's children, looked most like his mother, and, ironically, had been with her the shortest time. "Of course, it's yours. As soon as the holiday season is over, we'll build a trophy case in your room. You'll probably be winning a lot more awards."

"Will I have as many as Adam?"

"A little sibling rivalry?" Darcy asked.

"A *lot* of sibling rivalry," Luke leaned toward her and answered in a lowered tone. "Scott tries so hard to catch up." To the boy he spoke in a louder voice. "If you keep raising animals for the fair and if you participate in as many sports as Adam, you should be able to keep collecting prizes. It doesn't matter if you have as many as Adam as long as you're doing your best and having fun."

"Dad..." Scott admonished. "You always say that."

Darcy laughed. "I don't think that's what he wanted to hear."

"I've reached a point in fatherhood where nothing I say is what they want to hear," Luke told Darcy, then tousled his son's hair affectionately. "It looks like you need to change your turkey's water." He looked up and saw Adam and Greg approaching at a leisurely pace. "Hey, you guys. Hurry up. We don't want to miss the baking awards."

Luke glanced at Darcy. This whole scene must be pretty boring to her. She was probably used to spending her evenings discussing politics and the stock market instead of standing in a barn, surrounded by poultry. To his surprise, she seemed genuinely interested in the conversation.

"Darcy, you haven't met my kids yet, have you?"

"Not officially, except for Scott." She gave the boys a wink.

Luke made the introductions, watching his sons' reactions with interest. Scott accepted Darcy with his usual unquestioning friendliness. Adam was more cautious, but after a quick appraisal, he returned her smile. Only Greg held back, passing a flashing glance from Darcy to his father and back again. He said all the right things and was stiffly polite, but his lack of enthusiasm was evident.

But Darcy's smile never wavered. "Congratulations on all your ribbons. I don't know much about turkeys, but these look like fine specimens."

"Thanks." Adam and Scott spoke simultaneously, making no effort to stifle their pride of accomplishment.

Greg was apparently not as impressed with Darcy as his brothers were. Instead he pointedly turned away from her and faced his father. "Dad, I'm meeting Dave and Brian as soon as I finish here. Is it okay if I ride home with them?"

"If you promise to be home by ten."

"Ah Dad, we're not going to get into trouble. And it's not a school night."

Luke sighed. It was so difficult to let his sons grow up. "Okay, you can stay out until eleven. But get Brian to drive carefully. And wear your seat belt."

"Dad..." This time it was Greg expressing his disapproval.

"As soon as you finish here, come to the home economics building so you can see your grandmother win a prize or two of her own," he told his sons. "Scott, you stay with your brothers and don't wander off. And Adam and Greg, keep an eye on Scott—"

"Dad!" All three boys interrupted with great annoyance.

Luke threw up his hands in defense. "I'm leaving. Let's go, Darcy. We have just enough time to walk through the cattle barn."

She was chuckling as she matched her steps to his.

"I guess I'm going to have to get a whole new set of fatherly advice lines," Luke said wryly. "I think my old ones have been used once too often."

"I can remember my mother saying the same things to me."

"So can I. And it's a really strange feeling to hear myself repeating all those cautions I used to hate to hear." Luke dodged a still-fresh animal deposit and accidentally bumped against Darcy. His arm automatically went around her waist to steady himself. The fresh, spicy fragrance of her perfume drifted into his nostrils, pushing aside the sharp, earthy odor of the cattle barn. The pressure of her slender body against his sparked a surge of sensations he hadn't felt in years.

"Even though I know I'm in my mid-thirties, I don't feel any older than I did when I was Greg's age," he continued. "I look at my kids and see them growing up, but I just can't believe I'm getting older, too."

Darcy nodded. "I know what you mean. When I was a teenager, I never missed this fair. I remember how much my friends and I looked forward to the rides, the game booths, the food . . ." she paused and slid him an unintentionally provocative glance ". . . and the boys."

Even though he knew she wasn't actually flirting with him, the warm sparkle in her electric blue eyes swept him back twenty years. He and Darcy could have been teenagers on a first date. The soft evening breeze trickled through her long, glorious auburn hair, lifting it away from her face and spilling it over her shoulders.

Her hair had been the first thing that had caught his eye when he saw her. Dark, almost burgundy strands mixed with vibrant copper ones in a striking combination that brought an unexpected and almost irresistible urge for him to reach out and see if it could possibly be as soft as it appeared to be.

But his fingers were perfectly happy where they were. Beneath the short, fringed hem of her leather jacket, his hand curved around the side of her trim waist. Hormones he'd forgotten he had made his palms sweat and his heart rate falter, then surge with alarming irregularity.

Darcy could have stepped away. She could have broken the invisible tie that was holding him enraptured. But she seemed as caught up in the moment as he was. There was a hint of surprise in her eyes...and a spark of interest. There was nothing about the way she was looking at him that reminded him he was a responsible father of three and a man who had no time in his life for romance. Nor did it make him think of how temporarily she would be in Iowa. Because, at the moment, the only thing that mattered was the rush of youthful excitement he was feeling. And, for the first time in years, he was able to focus on his own interests as if he had no one else depending on him.

Luke and Darcy waited until a line of neatly shorn sheep and their handlers crossed the walkway on their way to the show arena. Then, slowly, reluctantly, Luke let his hand fall away and Darcy shifted so that their bodies were no longer touching as they began walking again.

The tour of the cattle barn was slowed when Darcy and Luke stopped to talk to several acquaintances who were either showing their animals or looking at the livestock.

"We're going to have to hurry or we'll miss the announcement of the winners," Darcy declared after a glance at her watch. "And if there's one thing that means a lot to my mother, it's these baking awards."

"I guess you don't see this kind of thing in California, do you?"

"I don't know about the rest of the state, but the L.A. area doesn't put much emphasis on baking prowess."

Luke was afraid to ask just what sort of prowess L.A. admired. It was a world he knew nothing about... and one about which he didn't care to learn. He didn't want to think how Darcy fit in there. Although she was nothing like the social snob he'd expected, he still couldn't forget that she was merely biding her time, anxiously counting the days until she would be leaving Greenhaven. It would be very foolish of him to spend any time wondering how things would be if Darcy wasn't going back to California soon. It would be very foolish of him to let himself care.

"THE JUDGES HAD a tough time this year. There were so many good entries that they had to go back for seconds and thirds." The rotund man at the microphone patted his prominent stomach. "It was a great sacrifice, but someone had to do it," he joked.

"Come on Stan, announce the winners," a voice from the crowd shouted.

"I'm building the suspense," Stan quipped back.

"You're going to make us miss the dance," someone answered. "I can hear the fiddles tuning up already."

The crowd began murmuring, drowning out the screeching moans of the band testing their instruments in the show barn next door.

"Okay, if you folks would rather go dancing than talk about food..."

"Yes, we would," a man interrupted, but a group of women booed him to silence.

"I'll go directly to the top prize," Stan continued. "Only twice in the sixty-five-year history of this fair have we had someone who could bake such an incomparable apple pie that she should be permanently honored in our Hall of Fame." Another murmur rose from the crowd, but this was more from an interest in the contest than from restlessness.

"I personally tested this entry, and I agree that it's the best apple pie I've ever tasted." Stan made a big production of looking around the room until he spotted the winner. "Her name will be engraved on the plaque at the county courthouse, but tonight she gets to take home this beautiful trophy. Will Mrs. Betty Carson please come forward and accept her prize?"

Thunderous applause filled the small building as Darcy's mother hugged J.W. before making her way through the well-wishers to the front of the room. Luke joined in, but his gaze was searching out his own mother. He knew she would be glad for her friend's victory, but she would also be disappointed. She had so few personal goals.

When Luke had a spare moment to think about it, he often felt a little guilty that he couldn't offer his mother a more exciting life. She had worked hard, helping his father build his construction business and raising Luke. Now, when she should be sitting by a lake taking it easy with her husband, she was living in a hectic household, once again cooking, washing and cleaning up after little boys.

Luke led the applause as the judge placed the red second-place ribbon in front of Nell's pie. He finally spotted her at the edge of the crowd accepting congratulations from some of the other entrants, including Darcy's mother.

"There are the happy bakers." He pointed them out to Darcy. "Let's go congratulate them."

She nodded and began edging her way through the crowd with such practiced skill that Luke had to hurry to keep up. But his height advantage over the people in front of him allowed him to see his mother give Darcy's mother a nudge and an optimistic smile when they saw he and Darcy were still together. So much for chance having anything to do with the evening.

Darcy was forced to stop suddenly, but Luke didn't notice in time to halt his forward momentum. The unexpected pressure of her firm buttocks against his thighs jerked his thoughts back to Darcy. As much as Luke hated to admit his mother might be right about his pathetic social life, he was enjoying the change of pace...and the change of companions. He enjoyed spending time with his sons, but he hadn't realized how much he missed being with an attractive woman and having an adult conversation with a female other than his mother.

"Darcy...Luke...did you hear the announcement?" As if there could be any doubt that she won, Betty cradled the large trophy in her arms like a baby.

"They're going to put my name on a plaque at the courthouse. Can you imagine that?"

"You'll be right there next to the lists of retired judges and war heroes," Nell added, her voice lowered with awe.

Luke's gaze met Darcy's, and they exchanged indulgent smiles.

"So, are the two of you having a good time?" Betty asked.

Abruptly, Luke and Darcy looked away from each other.

"We've spent most of our time with the boys in the turkey barn," Luke answered, carefully evading the real question.

"Adam and Scott are going to meet me in front of the Ferris wheel in an hour," Nell commented. "I'll let them ride a few rides, then I'll take them home."

"You don't have to do that, Mother," Luke said. "I'll watch them."

Nell waved him away. "No, you go out and have some fun yourself."

"And take Darcy," Betty piped up. "She's always loved these fairs. But don't take her on the Bullet. Why, I remember one time Bob talked Darcy into riding with him and she had just eaten a great big hunk of cotton candy—"

"Mother!" Darcy interrupted with a horrified exclamation. "Don't you dare tell that story."

"Oops, sorry. Well, surely I can talk about how you used to beat all the boys at the softball throw booth." Betty smiled fondly at her daughter. "I remember how your room used to be full of stuffed animals."

Darcy's wide eyes took on a desperate gleam as she grabbed Luke's arm. "I think we'd better hurry if we want to visit the horse barn before they draw the curtains on the stalls."

"Uh...yes. We don't want to miss seeing the horses," Luke agreed, as anxious as Darcy to get away. It was only a matter of moments before his mother launched into his childhood misadventures. "I'll see you at home later, Mom."

"Don't hurry. The boys will be fine with me," Nell assured him.

"Dad and I plan on going to bed early, so don't worry about us." Betty contributed her not-so-subtle encouragement. "We'll leave the front door unlocked."

Darcy leaned over and kissed her mother's cheek. "I'm really glad you won, Mother. We'll talk later," she added ominously.

Luke nodded. "You, too, Mom," he promised.

"I hope it won't be tonight," Nell commented, feebly trying to hide a yawn. "I plan on going straight to bed as soon as the boys and I get home."

Again Darcy led the way through the dwindling group of people in the home economics building and threaded into the growing crowd moving in every direction outside. She paused in the doorway and gulped in a deep breath of the cool night air.

"I'm so sorry. My mother is determined either to get us together or to embarrass me to death." Darcy looked up at Luke with an apologetic smile.

"I know what you mean," Luke answered with a sympathetic sigh. "Why do they have to push so hard?

It's not like I *have* to fall in love in the next twenty-four hours or live the rest of my life a lonely bachelor."

"Right. Falling in love isn't something that can be planned. It'll happen when it happens, and not because my mother thinks the time is right."

Luke opened his mouth to reply, but couldn't seem to focus his thoughts as he stared down at Darcy. The colorful glow of the midway danced through the gently shifting strands of her auburn hair. The stars seemed to be caught in the crystal blue depths of her eyes as she waited for his response.

"I've got my career and you've got your family," Darcy continued, but her beautiful voice was softer, even faltering slightly. "Neither of us needs a permanent relationship right now."

A group of passing teenage boys got into a good-natured shoving match and one of the boys backed between Darcy and Luke, shattering the intensity of the moment.

"Hey, I'm sorry, ma'am and..." the teenager blushed as he apologized "...Mr. Calloway! Hey, Greg, it's your dad."

The teenagers instantly regrouped around the two adults with Greg the only one hanging back. They were all staring with open curiosity at Darcy, waiting for an introduction that Greg seemed determined not to make.

Luke's eyes narrowed as he studied his son's sullen expression. Lately that was the attitude his son took about almost everything. He and Greg had always gotten along fine until the last couple of years. Assuming it was merely a phase Greg would grow out of, Luke was trying to be patient. But rudeness was one thing he refused to tolerate.

"Greg, why don't you introduce your friends to Miss Carson?"

Greg frowned, but he must have noted the determination in his father's eyes because he mumbled, "This is Darcy Carson . . . she's a newscaster in California."

The last part was obviously unnecessary as Greg's friends greeted Darcy with an avalanche of questions about Los Angeles, the beach, the cars, and of course, the movie stars.

Greg hesitated a minute, then punched the shoulder of the guy nearest him. "Let's get going, Dave. We don't have much time, and we still haven't ridden the Twister."

Reluctantly, the boy named Dave nodded and tugged on the arm of one of the other teenagers. "Come on, Paul."

One by one, the kids said goodbye and joined Greg who was gradually drifting away.

Luke started to call after his son, reminding him of his curfew, but stopped before he spoke. Greg was well aware of the rules, and it wouldn't make him any more cooperative for them to be reviewed in front of his friends.

Instead, Luke looked at Darcy and smiled. "You were a big hit with those boys."

"All of them but your son," Darcy pointed out with an intuitiveness that must have helped make her a top reporter.

"Sorry." Luke sighed. "I just don't know what's going on in his head right now. We seem to have lost touch."

Darcy shook off his apology with a shrug. "It's a teenage disease. He'll outgrow it. My brothers did and they were the most obnoxious creatures on this earth when they were sixteen."

A strange, carefree feeling swept over Luke. There was something in the lilt of her smile or the twinkle in her eye that lifted the worries away. The challenges of raising three sons as a single parent and the hard work of running a successful business would still be around tomorrow. But for tonight, Luke could almost believe he was young again. For a few hours he could forget his responsibilities and concentrate on this woman . . . this fascinating woman who was not really a date, but about whom he was already having thoughts that were dangerously delicious. Just for a moment, he could let his imagination run wild with the possibilities.

Impulsively, he took her hand. "Speaking of your brothers," he announced, "let's go throw some baseballs. I've always wanted to be with a woman who could win me a teddy bear."

AN HOUR LATER, Luke had two huge stuffed animals in each arm and Darcy was carrying a brandy snifter with a goldfish sloshing around inside.

"I suppose I should be intimidated by a woman who can throw better than me, but I guess I was forewarned."

Darcy laughed. "It's a skill that comes in handy in a newsroom. You have no idea how many stories I've wadded up and tossed across the room into a wastebasket."

They paused at a snack booth and Luke began juggling the toys in his hands in an attempt to reach his wallet. "All this exercise has made me thirsty. Can I get you anything?"

Darcy set the brandy snifter on the counter and pulled a five-dollar bill out of her purse.

"Why don't I buy this round?" she offered. "I'd hate to separate you from your teddies."

"It's been a long time since I touched a teddy," Luke responded, one dark eyebrow lifted suggestively.

Darcy tilted her head as she looked at him. "You look like a man who wouldn't forget how to take care of one."

"Uh hmm." The man at the counter cleared his throat. "May I help you?"

"I never let my dates pay for food," Luke stated, ignoring the interruption. He began shifting the plump animals in an attempt to reach his wallet.

"This isn't a date," Darcy reminded him. "We're just delivering pies, remember?"

He hesitated, then flashed her a resigned grin. "In that case, I'll take a large Coke."

"That'll be one large Coke *and*..." the man prompted hopefully.

"A small lemonade for me." Darcy took two straws from the dispenser and inserted one into each drink as they were placed on the counter.

But once again Luke was faced with the dilemma of having no free hands with which to hold his cup.

"Here, let me." Darcy took his drink and held it up. His lips closed around the straw and his cheeks drew in as he pulled the cold liquid into his mouth. Suddenly, the simple action became unintentionally sensuous, and Darcy's lips parted as she watched him. Their gazes met over the rim of the paper cup and Darcy felt her fingers tremble at the intensity of his eyes. The stormy gray color had taken on an intriguing greenish tint. Somehow, the change added a warmth that was both friendly and extremely sexy.

Slowly he took another drink and swallowed, drawing Darcy's gaze to the masculine bob of his Adam's apple in the center of his tanned throat. She pulled the glass away, then reached up to wipe away the moisture left behind. The tip of her index finger followed the curve of his lips, lingering a little longer than absolutely necessary.

"Is that better?" she asked, her voice sounding as breathless as she felt.

"Well, I'm not thirsty anymore," he answered, his tone husky as if his throat was still dry.

Darcy could certainly understand that feeling because her own throat seemed to have closed completely.

"Excuse me," the refreshment man cut in once again, "but could you move your fish? I have customers waiting."

Darcy and Luke looked around and saw that there were, indeed, several people waiting in line behind them, observing the interchange with mixed reactions. Most seemed amused, but there were a couple of teenagers who looked annoyed that their wait was being lengthened by two old people who should have known better than to make public spectacles of themselves.

Luke jostled the plush animals into a more comfortable position and muttered, "Let's head for the truck. Can you carry the drinks?"

Darcy, who had witnessed shocking behavior of all sorts around the world without a tinge of embarrassment, felt her cheeks flush hotly as she gathered the brandy snifter into the curve of one arm and picked up the two paper cups before following Luke.

When they reached the truck Luke started to put the animals on the hood, but Darcy stopped him with a pointed look at the thick coat of dust and God only knew what else that covered every square inch of the vehicle.

"I can't reach my keys," he informed her.

Darcy set the drinks and the brandy snifter on the flattest part of the hood, then said, "Okay, either pass me the animals or tell me where your keys are and I'll get them."

Sparks skittered across the darkness of his eyes, and Darcy could feel the heat of his gaze across the mound of stuffed toys.

"I never let a woman put her hands in my pocket on a first date." One corner of his mouth lifted in a teasing grin.

"But this isn't a date," Darcy repeated, enjoying the ongoing bantering.

Luke shrugged and all of the animals moved with the upward movement of his broad shoulders. "My keys are on the right side."

Darcy worked with dozens of men. She stood close to them and touched all but the most private parts of their bodies without giving it a second thought. But as her hand slid into the tight pocket of Luke's jeans, she was very aware of the warm-blooded body beneath the single denim layer. Her fingers became shy, gingerly seeking out the metallic safety of the keys.

She dared not look up because she sensed the strength of his gaze might completely unnerve her. Her hand was restricted within the confines, but she was able to reach the keys and withdraw them between the grasp of one finger and her thumb.

And not a minute too soon, she thought as she hurriedly turned her back to Luke while attempting to unlock the door. *Steady girl,* she admonished herself. *This man needs a full-time woman in his life, and that's the last thing you want to be.* She drew in a deep, calming breath and inserted the key. But before she turned it, she noticed the button was all the way up.

"We didn't lock the truck!" she exclaimed, whirling around to face him.

His expression was surprised, then he broke into laughter. "You know, I honestly forgot. I was so busy thinking about your hand in my pocket...well, you can imagine why I wasn't thinking too clearly."

Darcy couldn't keep from adding her own chuckle to his. She hadn't remembered, either, and her thoughts hadn't been any purer than Luke's. She opened his door, then walked around to her side where she had to jerk with all her strength to get her own stubborn door open. Luke positioned the toys on the seat while she settled the goldfish container on the floor, then handed him his keys.

In the bright light of the cab, Darcy lifted her gaze and caught Luke's eyes focused on her. She was vaguely aware of the lively sounds of fiddles and a wild piano drifting across the cool night air.

"I suppose we should go home now," Luke commented in his responsible-father voice.

Darcy's spirits drooped. Even though this wasn't a date, she realized she didn't want it to end. Against her better judgment, she had thoroughly enjoyed the evening. After the initial awkwardness, she had found it easy to be with Luke. Possibly it was because she knew their relationship would go no further, or maybe it was because there was no pressure on either of them. But she had, for the first time in ages, been able to relax and be herself.

"I haven't been to a country and western dance in years," she mentioned. However, beneath her casualness, she was studying Luke's reaction, feeling unusually vulnerable. When his soft, sensuous lips spread into a smile, her heart fluttered in her chest.

"Miss Darcy, ma'am, may I have the pleasure of escorting you to the dance?" he drawled as he executed a courtly bow.

Darcy tossed her hair back and heard something that sounded suspiciously like a giggle escape her lips. "It's a date, sir."

## Chapter Five

The show barn was filled with people, some standing around the arena talking while most swirled and stomped across the portable wooden floor that had been spread over the sawdust.

Darcy and Luke didn't hesitate, but joined the action as soon as they walked through the doorway. He held out his hands and she took them as they tagged onto the end of a line that was galloping through the Cotton-eyed Joe.

Laughing and breathless, they didn't step to the sidelines when the band changed tempo to a slower cowboy ballad. The lights in the big building dimmed as Luke held out his arms and Darcy moved into them, fitting against his tall, hard body as if she had been dancing with him for years.

Darcy leaned her head back until she could see his face. It was a nice face, strong, masculine and undeniably handsome. The pleasure sparkling in his eyes confirmed that he, too, was glad they had decided not to leave. The breeze had tousled his hair, making him look younger...not at all like a father of three children *and* a turkey farmer. Boy, had she been wrong about that preconceived notion.

"Having fun?" he asked, his voice low and intimate, his breath warm against her skin.

"Yes, I am," she admitted, more than a little surprised to realize it was the truth. But she couldn't resist adding, "But don't tell my mother."

His gaze caressed her face and his arms tightened, pulling her closer. "I don't think she'd approve of what I'm thinking right now anyway."

A flash of pure sexual longing twisted through her, leaving her shaken from its intensity. Weakly, she leaned against Luke and rested her head on his shoulder as she followed his lead.

She could feel his heartbeat under her cheek and the sharp edges of his belt buckle pressing into her stomach. And, as their bodies swayed and moved, she became aware of his own physical reaction to her. The dance positioned them intimately, making it impossible for her not to feel the bold bulge in his tight jeans. The molten core deep within her ached more with every step, and it was obvious that Luke was suffering the same torment.

Oblivious to their surroundings, Darcy lifted her face again, but this time his was mere inches away. Slowly, inevitably, he leaned toward her until he was so close her vision blurred. Her eyelids drifted closed as his mouth brushed across hers, gently, tentatively.

His lips had felt firm beneath her finger earlier when she wiped off the cola. But against hers, they felt surprisingly soft. The contrast between their tenderness and the hard evidence of his desire practically bruising her hungry flesh, even through the layers of their clothing, showed two totally different sides of the man's personality. In his arms Darcy felt comfortable and protected, yet he made her well aware he found her exciting.

Another change in the music pulled them apart, but their gazes remained locked as they shuffled through the Texas two-step. It was only with the greatest reluctance that they parted when an old acquaintance of Darcy's cut in. But Luke didn't seek out another partner, choosing to stand on the sidelines, his eyes focused on her, following her until the dance ended and he could claim her again.

It was after two o'clock when the band finally put down their instruments for the last time that evening. The lights resumed their full wattage, forcing the dancers back to reality. The romantic shadows once again became the uninspiring interior of a barn. The faceless figures that had swirled past were recognized as familiar neighbors and friends.

Darcy and Luke stood a step apart, putting a cushion of neutrality between them. But as they turned and began to walk wordlessly toward the truck, their fingers brushed together and somehow became entwined. Separate, they would have been jostled apart, but united, they had no difficulty maneuvering through the crowded walkways to the parking lot.

Luke glanced at Darcy as the truck's engine sputtered to life and backfired a couple times, drawing a dozen sympathetic stares.

"I'm sorry about this truck," he began.

Darcy settled the goldfish bowl on her lap and smiled at Luke. "No one could accuse you of trying to impress me."

With an unnecessary degree of concentration, he studied the narrow space that was illuminated in front of the truck by its headlights. His tone was casual as he asked, "So what would it take to impress you?"

Darcy sensed her answer might be very important to any future relationship, however temporary, that might exist between them. "Actually, I don't impress easily," she admitted.

"I guess you wouldn't. Living in L.A., you're surrounded by Mercedes and movie stars."

She glanced at him sharply. "That's not what I meant. Cars and actors don't impress me."

"Yeah?" he questioned skeptically. "What sort of car do you own?"

"Uh..." she hedged. "Well, that's not important...."

He challenged her with a steady look.

"Okay, so I drive a Corvette...."

"Red, I'll bet." He turned his attention back to the road.

"Okay, it's red," she conceded defensively. "So what? The station gave it to me. I wouldn't care if it was a Toyota."

Again, he pierced her with an unconvinced glance.

"All right, I'll admit it." She threw up her hands in defeat. The motion upset the brandy snifter, and she had to grab it to keep the fish from pouring onto the floor. "Yes, I enjoy driving that car. It's a great car.

But I'm not so shallow that I care what sort of car someone else drives."

"So you don't mind riding in this truck?"

She peered at the thick layer of dust on the dashboard and the worn blanket covering the seat. There were turkey feathers on the floorboard and a scattering of corn kernels as if a bag of feed had broken sometime in the ancient vehicle's questionable past. Then she looked over the fluffy barrier of stuffed animals to the man behind the steering wheel. Only hours ago, she had never seen that face. And now she knew she'd never forget it. It was the man, not the truck she found disturbing.

"No," she answered honestly. "I've ridden in worse. In fact, I learned to drive in a truck that belonged to my grandfather. But I will say that Gramps did wash his truck on occasion."

They turned into her parents' driveway and Darcy had to hold the brandy snifter up so the water didn't bounce out when they crossed the cattle guard.

"And you could use a new set of springs," she added.

A low, appreciative chuckle vibrated across the darkness. "Springs? This old pile of bolts wouldn't know how to drive if it had springs. Why, there probably isn't even anything left to attach them to."

He stopped the truck in front of her door, but didn't turn off the engine. When he began unloading the stuffed animals, Darcy reached out and pushed aside one of the panda bear's ears so she could see Luke.

"I don't need any more stuffed animals in my room. My mother seems to think everything should be left exactly as I had it.'' Darcy shook her head. She had long ago given up trying to convince her mother she wouldn't be moving back home. "Why don't you give them to your boys? Greg may be a little too old, but Scott and maybe Adam would give these guys a good home."

She nestled the brandy snifter in between a big bear and a fluffy dog.

"And the fish?" Luke asked.

"And the fish," Darcy confirmed, laughing at his unenthusiastic expression.

"Great. Thanks," he stated with good-humored sarcasm.

"Goldfish are terrific pets. They don't make any noise, and they never make a mess on the carpet."

"Or we can feed him to the turkeys."

"Luke!"

He held up his hands to calm her. "It's a joke. Besides, turkeys don't eat meat."

"I'll bet they wish more people felt that way."

"You're not one of the those animal rights' activists, are you?"

This time Darcy's chuckle was wry. "Funny you should mention that...animal rights is exactly why I'm on suspension, remember? But I was just reporting it, not participating. Actually, I can see both sides of the issue. I don't like to see animals tortured for unnecessary experiments, but I don't have a problem eating chicken . . . or turkey."

"So how long do you think it'll take to clear up your case?"

Darcy led the way up the porch steps and Luke followed. "My attorney thinks it'll go to court after Thanksgiving." She glanced back at the noisy truck. If he hadn't left it running, she would have invited him to sit for a while on the porch swing.

"That's a month away," Luke commented nonchalantly as he stopped with one booted foot on the top step.

Darcy turned to face him, and, because of her higher position found that they were eye to eye. "More or less," she replied. "But I don't know how long I'll be here. I have to fly back Monday or Tuesday for some depositions and the grand jury hearing, which means I'll be gone most of the week."

He thrust his hands deep into his pockets. "Then maybe I'll see you around."

"It's a small town." She responded with equal casualness, but inside she cried out, *But I wouldn't mind spending more time with you while I'm here.*

"Well...I guess I'd better be going," he said and backed down a step.

"I had a nice time this evening." *Don't leave. I want you to kiss me again.*

His eyes burned into hers, as if searching for an answer to an unspoken question. His gaze was so perceptive, Darcy began wondering if he might have heard her silent request. When he gave her one last little smile, then turned to leave, she felt her spirits droop with disappointment. On the dance floor, there had been a flash of magic. Had it been a fluke? A reaction to the circumstances around them? A moment of madness?

All she knew was that she wanted to feel his lips on hers one more time and to have him hold her tight in his arms. "Luke..." She moved toward him just as he wheeled around and bounded up the steps two at a time.

"Darcy..." he breathed as he cradled her face in his hands and covered her mouth with his. "I must be crazy," he muttered against her lips an instant before they crushed against hers.

Darcy's arms wound around his neck, her fingers feathering into the soft, dark hair at his nape. The banked fires that had built and died back...but never out...roared to life again. It had been a long time since a man's kiss had affected her so much. Her body molded to his, automatically seeking the boldness of his response.

If she hadn't been standing on her parents' porch...if he hadn't been a widower with three kids...if she hadn't been so anxious to get on with her life in California...if he hadn't been a livestock farmer...she would have asked him to turn off his truck's engine, rev up his own engine and stay for the night.

Then, as abruptly as he had approached her, he let her go. After one last, lingering look that took away what little strength she had left in her knees, he pivoted on his heel and vaulted down the steps.

Darcy leaned against the heavy support post at the top of the steps and watched him leap into his truck, grind the gears into reverse, then head toward the road. She realized her hand was clenched against her chest as if she was trying to steady her rampaging heart. Somehow she knew that kiss would come back to haunt her during the long, lonely nights in her bed in L.A.

Luke's truck blasted a farewell backfire that took away her last hope that her mother wouldn't know what time Darcy's evening ended.

"Terrific," Darcy muttered. As if she wouldn't have enough trouble discouraging her mother's matchmaking, Darcy knew it would be difficult to muster a genuine objection.

"AND AS THE holiday season approaches, we get so involved with ourselves that we forget about God. Remember that He has a plan for us even though sometimes we might get a little sidetracked...."

"Dad, Adam touched me."

Luke leaned toward Scott and whispered, "Tell Adam I said to keep his hands to himself."

Scott obediently relayed the message and Luke gave Adam an "I really mean it" look. Adam responded with a dirty look directed at Scott, then scooted closer to his grandmother.

Luke heaved a fatherly sigh and wondered if he'd survive until his kids reached adulthood. With one last pointed look at Adam, Luke turned his attention back to the pastor who was just getting into his sermon.

But his good intentions were forgotten when the sight of Darcy filled his vision. She was sitting with her family at the opposite end of the row in front of him, far enough away that he couldn't hear her voice during the song service, but close enough that he could see the long, dark curl of her eyelashes and the sedate pearl earrings peeking through the shiny curtain of her hair.

Such beautiful hair. The memory of its softness against his cheek was still fresh enough to make his skin tingle.

And her eyes. A man could be hypnotized by their crystal blue twinkle and never know what hit him.

He couldn't list her assets without including her voice. It was smooth as warm molasses with an intimacy that she must have learned in broadcasting classes.

And what a body! He'd never seen anyone fill out a pair of jeans like she did. The memory of her breasts pressed against his chest and the softness of her stomach that had cushioned his arousal brought beads of perspiration springing out on his forehead. For a few hours, she'd made him forget that he was a responsible adult, parent and pillar of the community. With Darcy all he could think of was that he was a man…a man who wanted to see that body without jeans and feel that hair against his bare skin, a man who wanted to bury himself in her warmth and hold her in his arms until their passion was spent.

Guiltily, Luke jerked his gaze away from Darcy and glanced around at the other members of the congregation, afraid someone might have been able to read his less than saintly thoughts. As unobtrusively as possible, he wiped the back of his hand across his brow and forced his attention to the sermon. It was obvious he was going to need divine help to keep his mind off the tempting woman in the next row.

In fact, as much as he'd like to explore the possibilities, Luke knew the only way he'd be able to not think about Darcy was to keep away from her. Soon she'd be back in her jet-set L.A. life-style and things around Greenhaven, including Luke's libido, would return to normal.

Unfortunately, normal for Luke meant a nonexistent sex life. He hadn't been with another woman since Ellen's death, so it was easy to see why his hormones had gone wild at the slightest stimulus. It was good that Darcy came back to town. She had helped Luke realize he was still a healthy male with normal sexual appetites. Perhaps it was time that he started thinking a little more about himself.

Again, he glanced around the church, settling briefly on each of the eligible women in the congregation. There was Sandy Johnson whose husband had run off with his secretary a couple of years ago. She wasn't a beauty, but her roots were firmly planted in Iowa soil. And there was Annie Wills, an elementary-school teacher who had never married. She would certainly be good with his kids. Then there was Renée Nelson who had three children of her own. Renée's husband had died only a year ago, but already she was letting it be known that she didn't like the single life and was wanting to remarry.

Luke's survey screeched to a halt when a silky fall of burnished copper hair came into his line of view. And then there was Darcy, beautiful, intelligent, fun to be with. However, while she wasn't married, she was definitely not eligible.

No, it wouldn't be a good idea to spend any more time with Darcy. He was practical. Anyone who raised livestock had to be. So if he was going to jump back into the dating game, he wasn't going to be foolish enough to fall in love with a hummingbird or a peahen. He needed a practical, down-to-earth bird like the turkey.

"I'M GOING TO DRIVE into town and do some shopping, Mother. Do you want me to pick anything up for you?" Darcy took her leather jacket out of the coat closet and fished her keys out of her purse. Darcy had just returned from California with her own car yesterday and was anxious to get out and run some errands.

Betty leaned around the kitchen doorway and answered, "Yes, would you buy a couple bags of candy? Tonight's Halloween, you know."

"You don't get many trick-or-treaters out here, do you?"

"Not many, but those who go to the trouble should get some nice treats. Buy something good like those little candy bars."

"Anything else?"

"Well, there are one or two things I need for lunch tomorrow. Let me write them down."

A few minutes later, Darcy slid behind the wheel of her Corvette, the list safely tucked into her purse. As much as she'd tried to deny it, she loved the power and prestige of the extravagant machine. The feel of the leather wheel in her hands and the narrow pedal beneath her foot was more satisfying than most of the men she had dated in the last ten years.

She could think of one man who might be the exception, but she shook him out of her thoughts. It had been almost a week since she'd seen him in church. They'd exchanged polite "hellos," under the watchful eyes of their mothers and Luke's children. Darcy and Luke had quickly moved on to visit with other people. He'd made no effort to lengthen the meeting and hadn't tried to contact her before she left or since she returned.

Granted, he would have had difficulty reaching her since she'd flown to L.A. Monday morning, spent two long, exhausting days in meetings with her attorney, court reporters and the opposing attorneys as she gave her deposition, followed by innumerable questions from the grand jury. Thursday and Friday she'd been on the road, driving back to Iowa, arriving near midnight last night.

Warned by her attorney that the case probably wouldn't go to court until late November or early December, she'd returned to Iowa resolved to make the best of the situation and enjoy the holiday season with her family. It would have been nice to have Luke to help pass the time, but they were both probably better off to avoid a relationship that would surely become more physical.

Darcy drove down the main street, waving at several people she knew before turning into the Wal-Mart parking lot. The large discount store was a new addition to Greenhaven and had quickly become the shopping headquarters for all but the most specialized items.

She was pushing a cart through the store, studying her mother's list as she walked when she felt the cart hit something solid. Looking up quickly, an apology on her lips, her breath caught in her throat when she saw the object was Luke.

Turning, he seemed to be equally prepared to apologize for blocking the aisle, but stopped. For a full minute they stared at each other, hungrily, eagerly taking in every detail.

"Hi. Doing some shopping?" she was finally able to murmur, then groaned at the total inanity of her remark. Of course, he was shopping. What else would he be doing at Wal-Mart on a Saturday?

He held up a list similar to her own. "Last-minute party things. Greg and his friends are putting together a haunted house in our basement, and he ran out of spider webs."

"He should come to our barn. It's the Club Med for spiders. They travel from miles around to winter in the rafters."

"It sounds like *Arachniphobia.*"

His eyes were telling her he was glad to see her, but he was keeping her cart between them as if it was made out of impervious granite instead of wire mesh.

"No, actually, it's more like *Charlotte's Web.* I put on a production of that with all my friends one summer," Darcy said, wondering how Luke could look so gorgeous in a baggy black sweatshirt and faded jeans.

"Dad, they have fangs. I really need some fangs." Scott appeared around the corner and slid to a halt beside his father. "Oh, hi, Miss Carson. Thanks for the stuffed animals and the fish. He lives in my bedroom and watches out for monsters while I sleep."

"I didn't realize he was a guard fish." Darcy smiled down at the little boy.

"Yeah, he's terrific. I'm still trying to talk Dad into getting me a puppy, but Sebastian is a real nice pet. I named him after the crab in that mermaid movie."

"You want a puppy?" Darcy asked. "Then you should come visit my dad. His dog has eight of the cutest puppies you've ever seen, and they're about two months old and ready to find new homes."

Scott's big blue eyes widened even more. "Gosh, Dad. They have *eight* puppies. Could I have one? Please? I'll feed it and let it sleep in my bed."

"We'll talk about it later, Scott," Luke responded. "Now what about those fangs? I thought you were going to be a Ninja warrior. Since when do they have fangs?"

"Bye, Miss Carson," Scott called as his father guided him in the opposite direction. "I'll try to come see the puppies soon."

Luke gave Darcy an annoyed, exasperated look that might have made her feel guilty if she hadn't been so busy noticing how attractive he was even from the backside. If turkey farming could get a man into such good physical condition, then perhaps she should recommend it to some of the men in California. They were spending all that time and money working out with machines when she couldn't remember seeing a nicer pair of masculine buns.

It wasn't until Luke and his son disappeared down an aisle that Darcy could force her attention back to her mother's list.

*"TRICK OR TREAT!"*

Darcy watched her mother hurry to the front door with a big bowl of candy cradled in her arm. It was obvious that Betty got as much of a kick out of seeing the little kids dressed in their costumes as the kids got from receiving all those free goodies.

"Darcy, honey, come look at these children," Betty called. "They're so cute. There's even a Raggedy Ann."

Obediently, Darcy walked to the door and oohed and aahed over the costumes as was expected of her. Actually she did enjoy seeing them. It was a refreshing change to see these rural children with their homemade costumes instead of the elaborate wardrobe-department costumes the children wore who came to her door in Santa Monica. No one would have considered wearing an old sheet or her mother's party dress like they did here.

The group ran back to the waiting car and were driving away when another car drove up. Darcy leaned against the doorjamb, watching as two kids jumped out, followed by a slower, less enthusiastic parent. It wasn't until the man stepped into the circle cast from the yard light that she recognized Luke. With new interest, she studied the two kids, realizing they must be Adam and Scott.

Just in case she didn't recognize him, the littlest boy pulled up his black hooded mask and announced, "I'm Scott."

"Oh, I'm glad you told me," Betty said with a great show of relief. "I was afraid it might really be a ka-rate guy."

"I'm a Ninja warrior, but I don't hurt people . . . except my brothers."

"Yeah," Adam sputtered. "Like you can really hurt me."

"Boys, let's get our tricking and treating over with—" Luke began, but was interrupted by Scott's excited voice.

"So we can look at the puppies. Dad says we might get one."

Betty dropped some candy into their bags. "I have to stay here and guard the door. Darcy, why don't you take them out to the barn to see Jemima and her babies?"

Darcy and Luke exchanged uncomfortable glances over the heads of his sons, but there was nothing either could say without creating a scene. Darcy got her coat out of the closet and led the way across the yard with Scott skipping along beside her.

As soon as she opened the barn door and turned on the light the puppies and the boys found each other. Adam and Scott fell to their knees on the straw-covered floor while eight coal black, roly-poly puppies covered them with happy kisses.

"I was hoping they wouldn't like them," Luke muttered.

"Fat chance. Since when do kids and puppies not fall in love at first sight?"

His voice was low and much closer than she expected. "I suppose some things are inevitable."

Darcy pivoted slowly, sensing he was standing behind her... very close. Her gaze started at the neckline of the sweatshirt where a few dark hairs peeped over the ribbed band, then moved up to his confused gray eyes. "Maybe if you don't fight it, it'll run its course. They could get tired of the puppy and be glad to see it go," she said, knowing neither of them was really talking about the boys or the dogs.

A sigh, filled with the hopelessness of their situation, escaped from his lips. A tender, bittersweet smile lifted one corner of that sensuous mouth as he added, "I think they'll fall in love and never want it to leave. And I'm beginning to understand how that might feel."

# Chapter Six

The boys were busy with the puppies and didn't notice when Luke took Darcy's hand and pulled her behind the door of an empty stall. Nor did they notice when he gathered her into his arms and covered her mouth with his own in a kiss that expressed all the longing and loneliness he had been feeling all week.

He tunneled his fingers into the thickness of her hair, drawing her head back. Her lips were soft and full and tasted just as sweet as he remembered.

"I can't believe how much I wanted that," he whispered when they finally paused to catch their breath.

"Was one enough?" she teased. Her arms were circling his waist, holding him close and making no attempt to put any distance between their bodies.

His chuckle was raw with desire. "No, one just made it worse. I don't know how many of your kisses it'll take before I get enough." He nuzzled his face into the smooth skin of her neck. "But I'm willing to start counting now."

The tip of Darcy's tongue touched the sensitive curve of his earlobe and he groaned, knowing he wasn't just stepping into deep, dangerous water, but that he was diving in headfirst.

His head dipped lower, following the V-neck of her sweater with soft, lingering kisses. He heard her gasp and felt the acceleration of her heartbeat beneath his lips when he reached the shadowy valley between her full breasts. His tongue dipped down to taste her warm flesh as his hands moved to cup her breasts and lift them. He nudged the knitted material aside as his ravenous mouth searched for the nipple that had hardened beneath his fingers.

"I want this one...Dad, where are you?"

The childish voice pierced the fog of passion that had dulled Luke's senses. His head pulled back and for several seconds he and Darcy exchanged heated, frustrated looks.

"Damn," he muttered and gave her a shaky, crooked grin. Then, as he dragged his fingers through his hair and pulled the waistband of his baggy sweatshirt over the telltale bulge in his jeans, he stepped out of the stall and approached his sons. Never in his years of fatherhood had he so longed for his kids to be somewhere else, preferably miles away.

Scott was lying on the floor with a puppy standing solidly on his chest.

"See, he likes me," Scott announced with great pride.

"He just likes all the candy you've got smeared on your face," Adam pointed out with annoying practicality.

"Dad, can I keep him? Please...please." Scott drew out the last word into three pleading syllables.

Luke was so distracted that he barely heard his son. "Sure, take him to Mr. Carson and see if it's okay with him."

The boys stood and both tried to pick up the puppy at the same time with Adam grabbing the front paws and Scott left holding the puppy's back end.

"You're going to drop him." Adam tried to pull the dog away from Scott.

"He's going to be mine, so *I* get to hold him," Scott stated as he hung on.

"Adam, let your brother carry the puppy," Luke commanded, his patience running unusually low. All he could think about was Darcy who was still hiding in the empty stall.

"But Dad . . ."

Luke pointed to the door and commanded, "Go now or forget the puppy."

The boys looked at each other, at their father, then at the little dog. Adam must have decided taking the puppy home was preferable to arguing about who was going to carry it, so he let go. The puppy's weight was almost too much for Scott to handle alone, and the puppy hung over his arms as he headed for the door with Adam, Jemima and the seven other puppies following close behind.

Luke rounded up the dogs before they could escape through the opening and quickly shut the door behind his sons. When he turned around he saw Darcy leaning against one of the big posts that supported the barn's tall gambrel roof.

"I honestly forgot they were here," she admitted, her face still attractively flushed.

"Even worse," he admitted, "so did I. And I'm their father." He shook his head and shortened the distance between them, drawn to her like a june bug to a porch light. "Look what you've done to me...I can't think about anything or anyone else," he murmured against her uplifted face.

"Look what *I've* done! I should be concentrating on my case." She slid her hands inside his sweatshirt, fanning her fingers over his chest. "I don't have time for romance." Her tongue circled her lips, leaving behind a moist trail he found irresistible.

The tip of his tongue followed the same path before his mouth closed upon hers. Their tongues touched, teased, then mated in a passion that burned too deeply for either to ignore. Her hands moved around to his back and flexed like a happy cat, caressing his skin with her fingernails.

"Oh, how I want you." His voice was as ragged as his nerves.

"What is it with us?" she asked, obviously as bewitched and bewildered as he was. "It's like we're teenagers on our first petting date. I'm not usually this..." she paused, searching for the right word "...passionate. Honestly."

He nibbled on her lower lip. "Neither am I. You're the first woman I've even kissed since...well, for a long time."

"Maybe we're both just going through a vulnerable phase," she murmured, moving seductively against the pressure of his swollen groin. "One morning we'll wake up and it'll be over."

"I wish we could wake up together," he shocked himself by saying. "Uh...I mean..."

"Yes," she breathed, "I know what you mean."

Their lips met in a long, deep kiss that made him aware of every square inch of their bodies that was touching.

"Whatever happens," she said when their lips parted, "you know it's only temporary."

"I know." He kissed her again.

"I can't stay."

His mouth moved against hers as he murmured, "I know that, too."

"Not even if you ask."

His hand cupped her cheek and she leaned against his palm. "I won't ask."

She lifted her head until their gazes met. There was a strange emotion swirling in her blue eyes as she continued, "As long as that's understood right up front. I don't want any sad scenes when I have to leave."

It was something he could promise now, but what about in two weeks? What if they did finally make love and it was as wonderful as he imagined it would be? What if this feeling in his heart turned out to be love? Would he be able to let her go without regret?

But he knew she was right. Whatever they might have together could only be temporary. Was it better that they spend what time they could together and see what developed, or should they separate now while only their raging libidos would be hurt?

Luke leaned forward and pressed a tender kiss against her forehead. Whatever it was about her, he knew he wasn't strong enough to stay away, as long as she was only a couple of miles down the road. Once she was back in California, it would be easier to deal with her absence from his life. However, for the moment, she was happy to be in his arms and he wasn't fool enough to push her away.

"I'll even throw you a going-away party," he offered with a bravado he hoped he'd be able to keep. "A back-to-the-beach party."

"And I'll wear my bikini." Her smile was intentionally provocative.

"Oh God," he groaned.

"Don't blaspheme," she teased.

"I wasn't," he answered with a wry chuckle. "It was a sincere prayer for strength." He stepped back and caught her hands as they slipped out from the warmth of his shirt. "We'd better get back before the kid squad comes back and finds us in a compromising position."

"Between our mothers and your kids, we'll probably never have any time alone."

"Oh God," he repeated. "And yes, that was a prayer, too."

DARCY REALIZED she was humming as she dressed for church the next morning. How long had it been since she had hummed? She couldn't remember ever humming in L.A. It just wasn't a California thing to do.

She was downstairs and waiting when her mother came into the living room.

"My, my, are you anxious to hear the pastor's sermon today?" Betty asked.

"The sermon? Oh, yes, of course," Darcy answered, ashamed at her fib, but even more hesitant to admit the truth. If her mother knew how things were developing with Luke, Betty would get her hopes up and begin to think there was a chance her daughter might decide not to go back to L.A. Darcy didn't want her mother to get hurt, so it was better that nothing was said. After all, there wasn't really anything to say about her relationship with Luke. It was purely a physical attraction. It would burn hot and fast, then be over.

Darcy had never experienced anything like that, but she'd heard about it happening to other people. She'd always thought she was too strong and intelligent to let something so purely sexual dominate her thoughts. But then she'd never met a man like Luke before.

And a relationship based solely on physical attraction was all the more reason not to let her mother know about Darcy's change of heart. Betty wouldn't understand or approve of two people, even consenting adults, having a sexual relationship without considering marriage. Darcy wouldn't be surprised if Betty still believed her daughter was a virgin.

Actually, that wasn't too far from the truth. Darcy hadn't been a virgin since her freshman year of college, but she hadn't slept with very many men. There always seemed to be a better reason not to than there was a reason to take such an intimate step. But Darcy knew it was a subject that would cause her mother a great deal of distress, so it was better left undiscussed. After all, what did her mother know about wild, crazy passion?

"Where's Dad?" Darcy asked as her mother put on her coat.

"Oh, he had an early meeting at the church. Something about the Thanksgiving baskets for the needy, I think." Betty plucked a set of keys off the hook by the front door. "We can take his truck."

"No, thanks." Darcy gave an emphatic shake of her head. "I've had my required rural experience with a truck for this visit. We'll take my car."

Betty's eyes brightened. "Your car? Cool."

Darcy blinked. Had her mother just said *cool?* She must have been watching too much television lately.

The red Corvette slid into a parking space between a pickup truck loaded with hay and a Jeep filled with sacks of feed. Almost everyone was already in the church, but those who were still on the wide pillared porch stared openly at the flashy automobile *and* its equally flashy driver. Darcy felt their gazes on her as she walked beside her mother, but it was the kind of curiosity and interest she could handle. She had refined her reaction to an art...a friendly smile that somehow telegraphed that she was honored, but offered no hint of encouragement.

Sunday School was just letting out and the church's sanctuary was filling up. Darcy followed her mother to the pew where her family had been sitting ever since the new church had been built in the early 1930s. She glanced over her shoulder and saw that the pew behind her was still empty.

But there was no doubt when the Calloway family arrived.

"I'm going to name him Joe," Scott stated firmly.

"That's a stupid name," Adam retorted. "I've never heard of anyone naming a dog Joe. It should be something fierce like Raider or Tiger."

"I like Joe, and it's *my* dog."

"Hush boys. You're in church," Nell reminded them.

"It's still a dumb name," Adam muttered, always determined to get in the last word.

"Scott, you sit between Grandma and me, and Adam, you sit on my other side."

It took a lot of willpower for Darcy not to immediately turn around as soon as she heard Luke's voice. Instead, she waited until her brother Bob and his wife arrived and she had to shift to let them pass.

"Oh, hi," she said, addressing the Calloway family in general and trying very hard not to look directly at Luke. "How's the puppy?"

"He's just the best dog I've ever met," Scott declared.

"He howled all night," Luke interjected.

"He peed on the living-room rug," Adam added.

Darcy waved her hand. "Never mind. I'm sorry I asked."

Nell glanced from her son to Darcy, then smiled. "Why don't you come to our house for lunch today and see for yourself? I'm sure one of the boys would show you around the farm."

Darcy hesitated, no longer able to keep her gaze away from Luke as she searched for his reaction.

For a second, he appeared to be as startled as she was, but then that now familiar grin stretched across his handsome face. "Sure, why don't you? I might even let you help me with chores."

Her heart did a strange little flip-flop when he focused those intense greenish gray eyes on her. "Chores, huh? That sounds like an offer I should refuse."

"Don't let him intimidate you," Nell snorted. "Just don't ever, under any circumstances, let him hand you a shovel."

"You'll have lunch with us, won't you Miss Carson?" Scott asked. "I'll bet Joe will be glad to see you again."

"That sounds like a wonderful idea," Betty added her encouragement. "Your father and I were thinking about going to lunch with the pastor."

"I guess since I've been forewarned about the shovel, I'll come." Darcy forced herself to pivot in her seat so she was once again facing forward. But it was more difficult than ever to keep her mind on the sermon.

After church both families walked to the parking lot together.

"I'll take my car and meet you there," Darcy said as she unlocked the driver's side door. "I'm going to stop by my parents' and change clothes first."

"Wow, is that *your* car?" Adam asked, his fingers trailing over the metallic-flaked cherry-red fender with more reverence than he had shown in church. "Will you let me sit in it?"

"Me, too," Scott piped up. "I'll bet it goes real fast."

Even Greg seemed impressed, but was determined not to let it show. He hung back, but Darcy noticed his eyes gleaming as he let his gaze caress the car's long sleek lines.

"I'll give you all rides in it, but only one at a time."

"Me first," Adam quickly cut in.

Scott glared at his brother. "You're *always* first."

"Okay, Adam, you can ride to the farm," Darcy said, "and Scott, I'll take you for a ride after lunch. How about you, Greg?"

"Nah, I'm busy," he answered bluntly. As if annoyed that he'd been interested, he walked to the Calloway car and got into the back seat.

"Well, let's go, Adam." Darcy gave Luke, his mother and Scott a wave, slid into the car, then unlocked the passenger's door so Adam could get in. They both snapped on their seat belts before she turned on the engine. The Corvette's powerful roar attracted even more attention as she drove out of the parking lot.

"So, what grade are you in, Adam?" she asked.

"Eighth."

"Do you like school?"

"Are you kidding? *Nobody* likes school."

Darcy chuckled. "I take that as a 'no.' What do you want to be when you graduate?"

"Something that makes a lot of money. Maybe a lawyer."

"You don't want to stay and run the farm?"

"Are you kidding?" he repeated. "I don't want to raise turkeys. I couldn't believe Dad gave up his job and our house...we had a really big house in the city...and moved us way out here."

"Do you dislike it so much?"

Adam considered the question for a moment. "No, I guess not. It's just different."

"How about your brothers? Do they miss the city?"

"Oh, Scott was a baby when we moved here, so he doesn't remember anything else. But Greg misses his friends. I don't think he's too crazy about the farm, either."

They arrived at Darcy's parents' house and she parked in front.

"It'll take me only a couple of minutes. You can come in or wait out here."

Adam climbed out, too. "I think I'll go visit with the puppies, if that's okay."

"Sure, but be sure to close the gate. I've already had to chase them down once, and I sure don't want to have to do it again."

Darcy changed into a pair of black slacks and a bulky knit sweater, then returned to the yard where Adam was sitting, surrounded by playful puppies. As soon as he saw her, he got up and gallantly held the gate open for her when they left the yard.

"Thanks, Adam."

His smile was shy. He was obviously feeling much more grown-up than his thirteen years.

Nell was busy in the kitchen when they arrived. She turned down Darcy's offer to help, but the meal had been cooking while they were at church, so it was a simple matter to put it on the table. Scott was setting out the plates and Greg was following him, putting the silverware and napkins next to the plates.

"Whose turn is it to say the blessing?" Luke asked after they were all seated at the table.

"Why don't you say it today since we have a guest," Nell suggested.

They all bowed their heads as Luke said grace over their meal.

"Scott was peeking," Adam declared triumphantly as soon as the Amen was said.

"Adam was shining light in my eyes with his knife," Scott countered, picking up his own butter knife and demonstrating how Adam had reflected light on the broad blade and directed it across the table.

"Boys!" Luke reprimanded. But he didn't seem too upset at the exchange.

"They're not usually like this," Nell said, leaning toward Darcy.

"No, they're usually worse," Luke added with good-natured acceptance of his sons' childish high spirits.

The meal was noisy but pleasant as Adam and Scott vied for Darcy's attention by telling her bad jokes and stories about school. As soon as they were finished, Nell shooed Darcy and Luke outside while insisting that the boys stay inside to help with the cleanup.

"Are you ready for the grand tour?" Luke asked when he and Darcy were in the mudroom leading to the backyard. "I'm not sure if it's a good idea so soon after lunch, especially for a city slicker."

"I beg your pardon—" Darcy pretended to be greatly insulted "—I may live in the city now, but I still know my way around a barnyard. Besides, I believe I can say with all sincerity that there are more turkeys in L.A. than there are in the entire state of Iowa."

"I've dealt with the human variety, and I prefer the fine-feathered ones."

"It's an acquired taste, like sushi."

Luke flashed her a wry grin. "I like sushi...as long as it's cooked."

"After getting sick on some bad sushi, I have to agree with you." Darcy took her coat from a hook and put it on. "It's one of the hazards of the city that I've learned to avoid."

Luke studied Darcy's feet, then selected a pair of rubber boots. "These are Adam's, but I think they'll fit you."

Darcy looked for a place to sit down, but Luke took a step closer, backing her against the wall. There was a suspicious gleam in his eyes as he offered, "Let me help you."

He knelt in front of her and lifted her right foot. After pulling her suede boot off, he cradled her foot in his hands, gently massaging it. Darcy gasped at the tingles that ran up her legs from her toes. Her feet were usually very ticklish, but the feelings he was generating were surprisingly sensual. Slowly, methodically, his fingers made their way along her foot and up to her ankle. Just when Darcy was beginning to wish his caresses would go even higher, he reached for one of the rubber boots and eased her foot into it.

After repeating the procedure with her left foot, Darcy had lost all interest in going on a tour. What she wanted at that moment was for Luke's fingers to work their magic on other parts of her body. As he looked up at her, she wished he would kiss her with all the passion she could see welling in the dark depths of his eyes.

Agilely, he rose to his feet. His eyes never left hers and she followed his movement until she had to tilt her head back to avoid breaking the emotional connection. He reached out and combed her hair away from her face with tender fingertips.

"You missed your calling," she managed to say around her heart that seemed to have lodged in her throat. "You should have been a shoe salesman. Your female customers would be flocking into the store for your help with fittings."

"It's the fatherly instinct." One corner of his mouth twitched as he teased, "When they were younger, I got a lot of experience putting on their shoes."

"That wasn't a fatherly caress."

"It wasn't meant to be a caress." He shrugged, but his look held no apology. "I don't know what you do to me, but even the most innocent thoughts turn sexy when you're around. I have a feeling things could get out of hand very quickly if you were to stay here much longer." He took a step backward but continued to hold her gaze as he added, "I guess it's good for us both that your stay isn't permanent."

Darcy was beginning to wonder just how good it could be.

## Chapter Seven

"How many people work for you?" Darcy asked as she stood in the middle of a huge poultry house.

"Only one . . . me," Luke answered. "I added a lot of automation when I built these barns. The daily chores of feeding and watering for up to sixty thousand birds can be done relatively easily by one person. It's only when I have to do mass vaccinations or debeakings that I have to hire someone. Otherwise, I get the boys to help me move the turkeys from building to building or to load them for market."

Darcy looked around at the mass of white bodies that filled the room. "How many are in here?"

"I keep five to ten thousand turkeys in each of my six barns, depending on the time of year, and separated according to their sex and age. The toms are ready to market when they're nineteen to twenty-one weeks old, and the hens are ready in only sixteen weeks because they don't need as much protein and they're smaller. I try to plan it so I have a crop ready twice a year."

"But I would have thought Thanksgiving would be your big time of year."

"It used to be. At one time ninety-five percent were sold during November and December. But now about fifty percent of the turkeys are sold during the other ten months. Their meat has become extremely popular in the last couple of years because it's lower in calories and fat than beef or pork. The packers make it into cold cuts, sausage and every other type of meat product."

Darcy looked around at the constantly moving white mass and was almost overwhelmed at the prospect of taking care of so many birds, especially when the number was multiplied by six. "It looks like a full-time job even with automation. Don't you ever get tired of the smell and the noise?"

Luke sniffed the air and shrugged. "Smell? What smell?"

Darcy glanced at him and saw he was teasing her.

"Honestly, I hardly notice it," he continued, then leaned close to her. "But I will admit that your perfume has really made my nose realize what it's been missing."

The door of the shed burst open and Adam leaned inside. "Dad, Dad...come quick!" he shouted. "Scott's puppy's in one of the turkey sheds."

The noise of the door and the child's loud voice sent the turkeys into a panic. Fat white bodies vaulted into the air. But the qualities that made wild turkeys adequate short-distance fliers had long ago been bred out of their domestic cousins, and the big-bodied toms promptly fell back to the deep litter of wheat straw that was spread over the concrete floor. Even the choppy flapping of their wings could get them only a few inches off the ground, which caused their frenetic motion to be a combination of running and leaping as they rushed erratically around the room, accompanied by a frantic chorus of gobbles and yelps.

Luke and Darcy looked around at the pandemonium.

"Damn!" Luke muttered. "I'll have to deal with this later. First, I've got to get that stupid dog out of the other shed. I knew better than to let him have that puppy." He whirled on his heel and hurried out of the building with Darcy scurrying to keep up.

It was easy to figure out which building had been invaded. The door stood open and there was a racket inside that was even louder than the shed Luke and Darcy had just left. Luke's strides widened until he was jogging across the yard. But before he could reach the building, the little dog came trotting out with Scott chasing behind him.

Darcy would have felt relief if there hadn't been a small brown turkey hanging limply from the puppy's mouth. She glanced at Luke and saw his disgusted frown. He didn't stop, but ran past the dog, shutting the door before he pivoted and headed back toward his son and the puppy.

It was obvious from Scott's stricken expression that he knew he and his pet were in serious trouble. Scott called and tried to coax the puppy to him, but the little dog thought it was a wonderful game and avoided his new master.

Luke advanced on the dog and motioned for Darcy and Adam to move around and close in. Finally, surrounded in a loose circle and tired from his play, the puppy sat down and looked expectantly at the humans. Scott immediately rushed in and threw his arms around the dog's neck.

Darcy looked from the little boy to the angry father to the young turkey still being held in the puppy's mouth. Scott was sobbing out loud, huge tears rolling down his cheeks. Darcy wished she could think of something to say to defusc the tension. She'd been involved in reporting hostage situations and scenes where crimes were still in the process of unfolding. Always, she had been able to keep up an intelligent dialogue regardless of what was happening around her.

But at the moment, her mind was blank. She didn't know anything about handling children or furious parents, much less naughty puppies and dead turkeys.

The puppy opened his mouth and deposited the turkey on the ground. Darcy winced, afraid to watch as Luke took a stiff step forward.

Suddenly, the turkey leapt to its feet, stretched its wings and shook. Luke stopped abruptly, even taking a surprised step backward. As everyone watched, the turkey strutted up to the puppy and greeted him with an almost motherly peep.

''Well, I'll be...'' Luke's words trailed off.

The puppy bounced to his feet, gently took the turkey in his mouth and, again, the bird went limp. With his long black tail wagging cheerfully, the dog trotted into the fenced backyard where he should have been all along. Once there, he carefully placed the turkey on the ground and then waited while his new friend stood. Together they went to investigate the food dish.

Luke, Darcy, Adam and Scott all exchanged amazed looks. But it was evident from the noise that was still clearly audible in the two turkey sheds that the situation was not yet over.

"Darcy, you'll have to take that dog back." Luke raked his fingers through his dark hair and sighed. "A turkey farm just isn't a good place for a dog."

Scott's big blue eyes filled with a fresh flood of tears. "No, Dad. Don't take away my dog. I forgot to shut the gate, but I'll remember from now on. I'll watch him better. I won't ever let him out of the yard again. You won't even know he's around...I promise."

Luke shook his head. "I'm sorry, son."

Scott sniffled, but he didn't throw a fit. Instead, he straightened his back and bravely met his father's gaze. "Joe's a good dog. He didn't hurt any of the turkeys, not even Linda."

"Linda?" Luke asked.

"The turkey we were saving for our Thanksgiving," Adam explained.

Darcy's gaze lifted again to the small brown turkey who was now following Joe the puppy around the backyard. "You mean, you're going to eat *that* turkey?"

"Yes, but..." Luke's voice reflected his exasperation.

"Why *that* particular turkey? It's so...cute."

"Oh no, no, no." Luke shook his head. "That's exactly why I refuse to let the kids name those birds.

If they get too close to them, they stop thinking of them as livestock and start thinking of them as pets. I raise turkeys, not pets."

"Then maybe you should let Scott keep his dog," Darcy commented so that only Luke could hear.

One dark eyebrow arched as he considered his response. He drew in several deep breaths, apparently trying to calm down enough to think rationally. He glanced from Scott to the two animals in the yard, then to Darcy.

"I'm going to check on the turkeys," he finally responded. "We'll talk about this when I get back to the house." He directed his attention to Scott. "Go close that gate before Joe gets out again. And watch him so he doesn't hurt that turkey."

Scott and Adam didn't hesitate, but ran to obey their father.

"He won't, you know," Darcy commented as she and Luke turned and headed back to the first barn.

"Who won't what?"

"Joe won't hurt Linda."

"Stop calling her that."

Darcy shrugged. She gave up that point, but pursued her original statement. "Joe is a Labrador retriever. It's in his bloodline to retrieve without hurting the bird. My dad always said Joe's mother had the softest mouth of any dog he's ever seen, which means—"

"I know what it means," Luke interrupted. "But I can't have a dog who carries my turkeys around, even if he doesn't harm a single feather on their bodies. It's just not good business."

"But is it good for your son to have his pet . . . his *first* real pet . . . taken away from him just because he slipped up once? He's only six, you know."

Luke glared at her sharply. "I *know* how old my son is. And I don't need any advice about how to be a good father, especially not from you."

Darcy slid to a stop. "*Excuse* me. I didn't mean to interfere," she snapped with more than a hint of sarcasm. "Since I don't have any children, I couldn't possibly know anything about them, could I?"

"I didn't say that."

"No? It sure sounded that way." Darcy lifted her chin as she met his gaze. "Thanks for lunch." She pivoted stiffly and began stalking off. Over her shoulder, she added, "Call my father if you want him to pick up the puppy. I don't want to be accused of butting into your family's affairs." Then, before he could respond, she returned to the house, kicked off the boots, grabbed her own boots and purse and left a shower of gravel behind her Corvette as she drove away.

"I DON'T KNOW what happened, Betty. They seemed to be getting along great at lunch, then boom. Darcy left in a huff and Luke's been as grumpy as a bear just out of hibernation."

Betty balanced the telephone on her shoulder so she could talk and still leave her hands free to finish washing the dishes. "Darcy didn't say anything, but I could tell she was upset. Her cheeks were flushed and her eyes were shooting sparks when she got back from your house yesterday."

"Hmm...maybe that's a good sign. Flushed cheeks, huh?"

"Not that kind of flushed," Betty answered with a disappointed sigh. "She was furious about something."

"It had something to do with Scott's new puppy. No one's said anything, but the boys are avoiding Luke like they're afraid he's going to say something they don't want to hear." Nell clicked her tongue as she paused. "And the oddest thing is that there's a turkey in our backyard. No explanation. Just a turkey running around, playing with that dog like it was the most natural thing in the whole world."

"You have lots of turkeys."

"Yes, but we've never had one in the yard. Why, I even heard Scott call her Linda, and that's one of Luke's biggest no-no's."

Betty didn't really understand Luke's objection to the name Linda, but it didn't seem important enough to question. "So what are we going to do to get Darcy and Luke together? We can't let this one little argument discourage us."

"I don't know...I just don't know. I'm beginning to wonder if maybe my son isn't destined to a lonely life."

"How can he possibly get lonely with you and the boys around all the time?"

"Hmm," Nell repeated thoughtfully. "You might have a point there. I wonder what would happen if it was just him and the boys for a while. Maybe he'd realize how nice it would be to have a wife around."

"If all he needs a wife for is to take care of his children, I'm not sure if Darcy is the right woman for him. She needs romance. I want her to meet a man who will sweep her off her feet and make her remember she's a woman."

"I have another plan...."

"LOUISE FELL AND BROKE her leg." Nell looked up from the suitcase she was packing and gave her son a grim frown. "She needs someone to help her and asked if I could come stay with her for a while."

"Is she going to be okay?" Luke asked.

"The doctor said it was a clean break and it should heal eventually. He's just not sure how long it will take. But he does want her to stay off her feet for at least a month."

Luke was genuinely concerned. Louise was his mother's older sister and his favorite aunt. She was getting on in years, so he knew any broken bone could be serious. "Would it be better if she came here to recuperate?" he offered.

His mother snorted, "Here? With the boys running in and out? The noise would drive Louise crazy. Besides, the trip would be very hard on her." Nell folded a quilted robe and placed it in the suitcase. "I think it'll work out better if I stay at her house, close to her doctor and her things."

It suddenly dawned on him that Thanksgiving was only three weeks away. "Do you think you'll make it home for the holidays?"

Nell's hands stilled and she sighed as she peered up at him. "I don't know, Luke. I honestly don't know.

As much as I hate not spending the holidays with you and the boys, if Louise still needs me, I won't be able to come back in time for Thanksgiving. But maybe I'll make it for Christmas.'' She studied him quietly for a few seconds, then asked, ''Do you think you can handle the boys, the dinner...everything on your own?''

''Sure, no problem,'' he responded quickly and confidently. ''I'll be through with delivering the turkeys in a couple weeks, and the boys can do a few extra chores.'' He knew it wouldn't be easy, but he was sure he could handle his household and his children. After all, he was an intelligent, efficient, mature man. ''Don't worry about a thing. We'll be fine.''

A strange smile twitched the corners of Nell's mouth as she turned back to her packing. ''I can't tell you how relieved I am to hear that.''

''Are you going to take the train?''

''Actually, I was hoping you'd drive me there. I know it will take a day out of your busy schedule, but I really hate to ride the train. Especially with all the luggage I'm going to have to take for such a long stay. I hope to get caught up on my reading and I can get some sweaters knitted for Christmas, so I have to take enough yarn....''

''Okay, okay, I'll take you.'' He glanced at his watch. ''I'm going to get one more run to the processor in today, then we can leave early tomorrow morning.''

Nell nodded her agreement. ''I'll try to have dinner ready when you get back.''

Luke's shoulders were straight as he left the room, but as soon as he knew he was safely out of sight, he flexed his muscles and relaxed his posture so it reflected his exhaustion. The market was good this year and he'd been pushing himself to get his turkeys to the processor before his competitors. If his boys weren't in the barns helping him, he barely had time to say hello to them.

And now he had the added task of running the house, too. Luke stretched his tired muscles. He knew he could handle it. But it would leave him no time for himself.

Not that he needed any time for himself. It wasn't like he had a social life... which was exactly the way he liked it. A woman would only complicate his life.

Luke shook his head and took his keys out of his pocket. Who was he kidding? He had enjoyed spending time with a beautiful woman. He'd almost forgotten the thrill of a passionate kiss or how soft a woman's hair was or how delicious her skin smelled. For one brief shining moment, he had been able to imagine what life might be with the right woman.

The trouble was that Darcy simply *wasn't* the right woman. She had no intention of becoming a housewife. She knew next to nothing about children. She couldn't cook or sew and probably had no desire to pursue either household task. In fact, she was wrong in every way. Well, except that she could turn him on faster than any woman he'd ever met, including...and he felt a twinge of disloyalty to admit it...his late wife, Ellen. Darcy's kisses could almost make him forget all the negatives about their relationship. Almost.

It was probably better that things had stopped when they did. One more evening, one more caress, one more whiff of her perfume and Luke might have begun calculating how much it would cost to move his turkey farm to California.

But luckily, that temptation was no longer an option. He hadn't seen or spoken to Darcy since she left so abruptly last Sunday.

It had been the longest two days of his life.

DARCY PACED AROUND the living room, restlessly glancing through the titles of books that overflowed the bookshelves. She wasn't in the mood to read. She headed toward the kitchen, but stopped in the doorway. She wasn't really hungry. If she kept eating because she was bored, she would weigh two hundred pounds by the time her case came to court. And then it wouldn't matter if she won or not because her station wouldn't want her back.

She returned to the couch and collapsed on the cushions. A contestant spun the wheel on a game show, then looked at the half-completed puzzle.

"Ask for a *T,*" Darcy stated to the television set.

"Pat, is there an *S?*" the contestant asked.

"No, you idiot!" Darcy shouted. "I told you to ask for a *T*. Can't you see it's 'turkey trot'? That letter was worth one thousand dollars. You could have won..." Darcy let her head fall back against one of the plump crocheted pillows her mother had made. "My gosh, I'm yelling at the television. It's finally happened . . . I've lost my mind. I knew it was just a matter of time. . . ."

The ring of the telephone interrupted her tirade, and she jumped to answer it.

"May I speak to Mrs. Carson?" the female voice on the other end of the wire asked.

"Mrs. Carson isn't in. May I take a message?"

There was a momentary hesitation before the lady continued, "Oh dear. I'm the nurse at Greenhaven Elementary School and we have Scott Calloway in our office. He's running a slight fever and has been throwing up."

"Scotty's sick?" Darcy repeated, hoping it wasn't anything serious.

"Yes," the nurse confirmed. "Someone needs to come pick him up, but there's no answer at his house and Mrs. Carson is listed as the backup emergency person."

"I don't know where the Calloways are, but Mrs. Carson won't be back for a couple hours, so she can't pick him up."

"Lean over the pan, Scott. That's a good boy." The nurse's voice was distant as if she was holding the mouthpiece away. She sounded distracted when she returned, "What did you say? You can pick him up?"

"Uh . . . yes, of course I can," Darcy answered. For a moment she'd forgotten how small the town was. No school in Los Angeles would release a child to someone who wasn't preapproved on an official list. "I'll be there right away."

"Great. Just come to the office." Her voice grew distant again. "I'll get you a paper towel, Scott. Just lie down. Someone is on their way to pick you up."

The phone clicked and Darcy dropped the receiver back onto its cradle. She looked down at the white sweatsuit she was wearing and decided not to take the time to change into something a little dressier. She grabbed her coat and purse and hurried to her car.

Just in case Luke or his mother was outside and didn't hear the telephone, she stopped at his farm on the way. His wreck of a truck was parked in the driveway, but the wire-mesh trailer attached to it was empty. There was no sign of the late-model car she had seen him drive to church. It suddenly struck her that if he had a Cadillac, why had he driven that ratty truck to the fair? He must have really resented having to take her.

There was no answer when she knocked at the door, so she got back into her car and headed toward town. She hadn't had to ask directions. The entire school system was located together on a large parcel of land just inside the city limits. Darcy and her brothers had gone from kindergarten to twelfth grade there, progressing from building to building, passing on warnings to each about tough teachers and trying to avoid spending time in the detention hall. Darcy parked outside the elementary-school building and walked straight to the nurse's office.

"Hi, I'm Darcy Carson, and I'm here to pick up..."

The nurse turned around, a thermometer in one hand and a clean pan in the other. Her cap was slightly askew and there were spots of questionable substances splattered across the front of her white uniform. From the room behind her at least a dozen children looked up, hoping to see their parents' faces, then dropped back to their chairs in disappointment. Only Scott managed a weak smile and pulled himself up from the small couch. As soon as his place was vacated, four of the children dove for the prime spot and began to argue over who was the sickest and who deserved the couch.

The nurse glanced over her shoulder, then back at Darcy. She made a motion that she would have shaken Darcy's hand had she been able. "Miss Carson, it's a pleasure to meet you. We've heard a lot about your success as a TV reporter. You know how small towns are. No one has any secrets." The noise behind her grew louder, and she shrugged. "It's been a zoo around here. First there was Scott, and then half the school seems to have come down with this. It must be some sort of virus. I hope it's just the twenty-four-hour variety."

"Scott's father still isn't home. Do you think I should take Scott to the doctor?" Darcy asked, worried that it might be something more serious.

"Keep checking his temperature. It was just under a hundred degrees ten minutes ago. If it rises to one hundred two, then perhaps you should consider calling his family doctor. But this seems to be just an intestinal upset. You can call me if you have any questions."

That didn't sound too serious, but it also didn't sound too pleasant. "Thanks."

"I'd better get back to my other patients," the nurse said with a smile. "Just sign Scott out at the front desk. It was nice meeting you." With that, she went into the small office and began refereeing the scuffle that was still raging.

Darcy looked down at Scott's small pale face. "Well, Scotty, I guess it's just you and me."

He nodded, but looked so nauseated that Darcy hurried them through the signing-out procedure and then outside toward her car. Scott brightened slightly when he saw the shiny red Corvette sparkling in the sunlight.

"Oh boy. I get to ride in your car."

Darcy glanced at the white leather interior and wondered if there was a tactful way to ask a child not to throw up in it. But Scott saved her the trouble.

"I'll roll the window down in case I get sick. I wouldn't want to mess up your neat car."

She settled him on the seat and fastened his seat belt. "Thanks, Scott. I'd appreciate that."

His sweet smile made her ashamed that she had even considered something so trivial when he was feeling so bad. She reached out and rested the back of her hand against his forehead like she had seen her mother do countless times when Darcy and her brothers were young. Scott's forehead was warm, but not alarmingly hot, which relieved her fears somewhat.

"Okay, big guy. Let's get you home and into bed. Do you know where your dad and grandmother are?"

"They drove to Des Moines. She broke her leg and won't be well until Christmas."

"She? Your grandmother?"

"No, Aunt Louise. She's real nice, but we make her nervous, so Grandma's going to stay until she gets better."

Darcy shuffled through the overabundance of pronouns and assumed Nell would be staying with Louise for a while. She also calculated the time it would take for Luke to drive to Des Moines and back and knew he wouldn't be home until at least late afternoon. Darcy's mother was feeding the homeless in Council Bluffs, so she couldn't be contacted. It all added up to the unnerving fact that Darcy was on her own, for the first time in her life, with a sick child.

She'd nursed her co-workers through illnesses when the occasion arose, but there was something much more daunting about being responsible for a child.

Scott was good to his word and made it home before he threw up again. Darcy had never felt more helpless in her life than she did as she knelt beside the boy, one arm around his shaking body while she held a cold, wet washcloth to his forehead. When he was finally finished, she wiped his face, then carried him to his room.

He wasn't as heavy as she would have guessed, and she was able to hold him in one arm while she pulled back the Teenage Mutant Ninja Turtle comforter and matching sheet. Gently, she settled him on his bed and untied and removed his sneakers. She opened the drawers of his chest until she found a pair of pajamas, then helped him change.

"Will you be okay for a minute?" she asked after covering him up. "I want to find a pan for you in case you can't make it to the bathroom."

He nodded, but his eyelids were fluttering closed.

Darcy returned a few minutes later with an empty plastic garbage can and a clean wet washcloth that she placed across his throat. She remembered that that had always made her feel better when she had an upset stomach. After checking his forehead again, she pulled a rocking chair closer to Scott's bed, then took a book out of her purse.

But her attention was drawn to the small boy as he slept fitfully. He wasn't nearly as obnoxious as she'd always thought a six-year-old would be. And he actually had a great personality. She wasn't around kids that often, but those she had encountered hadn't been all that likable, her nieces and nephews included.

Darcy reached out and touched his face, still pale except for bright spots of color on his cheeks. With his blond hair, blue eyes, pale skin and freckles, he must not take after his father. Darcy guessed Scott must have gotten his coloring from his mother. Did that mean Luke preferred blondes?

Darcy reminded herself that it shouldn't matter to her. Luke's preference in women shouldn't be her concern. She had no claim on him.

He seemed to be getting over his grieving period and would probably want to remarry soon. And he would have no trouble finding an interested candidate. A man with Luke's sexual drive needed a wife. And his boys needed a mother. Especially Scott. It would be easy for any woman to love the little boy.

In that way, Scott was just like his father.

# Chapter Eight

"What are you doing here?"

Darcy looked up from her place on the bathroom floor where she was helping Scott get rid of the crackers he had eaten earlier. When she moved, Luke must have seen the boy because he crossed the room in two big strides and knelt down beside her.

"The nurse at school called just before noon. She couldn't reach anyone here and my mother was gone, so I picked him up," Darcy explained as she turned back to Scott and wiped his mouth. "His fever broke a couple of hours ago, but he hasn't been able to keep anything down. The nurse thinks it might be a twenty-four-hour virus."

"Scott, how're you feeling, buddy?" Luke asked, his eyes dark with concern.

"I feel bad," the boy murmured. "Darcy said I got a bug. She promised to stay until I feel better...." His voice trailed off as he leaned weakly against Darcy's arm.

Luke's expression reflected pure masculine helplessness. He glanced from Scott to Darcy, his hands lifted in an unconsciously vulnerable gesture. Darcy considered passing the wet washcloth on, but she felt sorry for the child in her lap.

"The other boys have been asking about dinner. I'll stay with Scott for a while longer if you want to cook something for them and do your chores," she offered. She had to admit she was pleased to see his self-confident bubble spring a slow leak. She was still a little angry at the way he'd turned on her when she'd been trying to help. But, sitting so close to him in the small room brought back the more pleasant memories of their time together. Whatever faults he had, she couldn't ignore how physically attracted she was to him.

He, too, seemed to have drifted off on another train of thought. With an obvious effort, he refocused on the situation at hand. "I'd appreciate that. I've been driving all day. I tried to hurry back, but there was an accident on the interstate. I hope you weren't too inconvenienced."

Darcy looked down at the sleeping child with genuine affection. "I didn't mind. Scott's a pretty special kid."

"Yes, I think so. He was an unexpected bonus, and now I can't imagine life without him."

She stroked Scott's damp hair back from his forehead. "You're a lucky man," she murmured softly, too low for Luke to hear. Louder, she stated, "You go ahead and deal with the rest of the family. I'll get him back to bed."

Luke nodded and smiled his appreciation, then left the room. Darcy waited until his footsteps faded away before she slid Scott off her lap long enough for her to stand. She gathered his limp body into her arms and returned to his bedroom. He was much heavier in his sleep, and Darcy realized she should have asked Luke to carry the boy. But for a reason she couldn't explain, she didn't want to let the boy go. Not yet. Taking care of him touched a part of her she hadn't realized existed ... a part of her that would be left behind once she went back to the real world.

Darcy covered Scott, then returned to the bathroom to clean it up and to rewet the washcloth. She sat next to the bed, her fingers entwined with Scott's as she watched the sun set through the window in his room. She didn't see many sunsets in Los Angeles, usually because she was at the station either getting ready to do the news or actually on the air. But even on her days off, it didn't occur to her to go out and enjoy the sunset. It simply wasn't a California thing to do. Everyone was too busy. There was too much going on. People out there had things on their minds other than such an ordinary pleasure.

As the sun melted into the tops of the trees and the sky soaked up the warm, mellow oranges and reds of autumn, Darcy acknowledged that there was nothing ordinary about it at all. She imagined it would be spectacular reflecting off the ocean's frothy waves and vowed to make an effort to spend more time enjoying the natural beauty of life.

"Would you stay for dinner?"

Darcy jumped, startled by the voice beside her. She glanced up at Luke and shook her head. "No, I'm not very hungry."

He didn't speak for a moment, but continued to stare at her with eyes that were filled with a hunger of a different kind...a hunger she understood, but didn't want to acknowledge.

"Darcy...I...thanks."

She stood and stretched, unaware until that instant that her muscles had gotten so stiff. She felt she deserved an apology, both for his attitude on Sunday and his hostile greeting earlier that evening. When none was forthcoming, she couldn't resist remarking with cutting sarcasm, "I hope I wasn't butting into your family. We single folks don't know anything about birthin' babies and raisin' kids, you know."

Luke's jaws clenched, effectively biting back either an angry response or an apology. "I never said that," he finally spit out defensively.

"Not in so many words." Darcy shrugged into her coat and picked up her purse. "But it really doesn't matter one way or the other, does it? I'll probably never have kids, so it's not a skill I need to develop."

"There are women who have both a career and a family."

"But they don't have time to do either well. I'd rather be really good at one thing, and the thing I've chosen is my career."

"Men don't have to make those choices," Luke commented. "We're able to cope."

"Sure you are, with the help of a wife or your mother. And I would hate to think a man wanted me just to have someone take care of his house and his kids while he pursued his career."

The chill in his eyes melted as his gaze met hers. "I can guarantee a man would want more from you than that."

"They always do." Darcy was surprised by the bitterness she heard in her voice.

Luke seemed unsure of how to respond. Without further comment, he stepped aside as Darcy walked toward the doorway.

"Tell Scott I hope he feels better soon," Darcy said, glancing over her shoulder at the small boy sleeping peacefully under his Ninja Turtle comforter.

"I will."

For a brief moment, her traitorous gaze moved to linger on Luke's tanned face. "See you around," she managed to murmur, then hurried down the stairs, anxious to be away from the whole family feeling that permeated the old farmhouse.

Adam was sitting on the couch watching a rerun of a family sitcom. He looked up curiously. He wasn't as open as Scott, but at least there was none of the hostility that Greg made no effort to hide. Adam seemed to be holding back, always observing, waiting to make his decision on whether or not there could be a place in his life for Darcy. Her Corvette had impressed him, but there was an emotional depth to his personality that would not be so easily reached.

"Are you okay?" he asked with disarming perception.

"Sure, I'm fine," Darcy answered, but couldn't explain the tears that suddenly filled her eyes. She was barely able to toss a "goodbye" to him as she turned away and practically ran the rest of the way to her car.

"HOW'S YOUR SISTER?" Betty settled on a flowered vinyl kitchen chair.

"Louise is fine," Nell answered across the telephone line. "The break wasn't as bad as I led Luke to believe. It's barely a crack, actually. She's in a little discomfort, but she can get around pretty well. However, it couldn't have happened at a better time. I was trying to think of an excuse to leave Luke alone with the kids for at least a month."

"Are you trying to make him realize he can't live without you?"

"Heavens no!" Nell sputtered. "I have no intention of spending the rest of my life taking care of him and the boys. As much as I love them all, I've raised my family. What if I were to meet a nice eligible gentleman?"

"Nell! You wouldn't remarry, would you?"

"Of course I would. I had a wonderful marriage. It just didn't last as long as Fred and I had planned. We were supposed to have a big RV and be traveling around together. Fred wanted to spend his days fishing and I wanted to sit under a tree reading or knitting or whatever. We'd worked so hard during our marriage, raising Luke, taking care of my father and his farm, starting Fred's business and keeping it going. He wasn't supposed to die before we had a chance to enjoy our freedom."

"Oh Nellie. I'm so sorry," Betty cried. "Sometimes I forget how lucky I am to still have J.W. I don't know what I'd do if I were facing my golden years all by myself. Even though my children would try to help, it wouldn't be the same. They're busy with their own families."

"Yes, well, I want Luke to find someone special to spend the rest of his life with. The boys will be gone in a few years, and Luke isn't getting any younger. I don't want him to be alone."

Betty leaned forward and peered around the kitchen doorway at her daughter who was sitting on the couch, intently watching the evening news. It was a daily ritual. She knew that Darcy was interested in world affairs, but this daily obsession was more than keeping up with current affairs. Darcy was studying the newscasters themselves and, no doubt, wishing she were back behind the camera. It was not something Betty would want to do, but she was, for the first time, starting to realize how painful the leave of absence was for her daughter and how desperately Darcy wanted to be working.

"I'm beginning to give up on him and Darcy ever getting together," Betty admitted to her friend. "I don't know whose fault it is, or even if it's anyone's, but she and Luke just don't seem to be hitting it off. She's counting the days until she gets back to work."

"It's nice that she has a career. I don't think my son would be interested in a woman who didn't have intelligence and pride in herself." Nell clicked her tongue in dismay. "But I wish she'd give motherhood a chance."

"*You* do," Betty retorted with a chuckle. "*I've* been wanting her to find a nice young man and have me some more grandchildren. But she seems totally immune to the appeal of a family. She spent most of yesterday over there taking care of Scott, but it was only because there was no one else available. She left as soon as Luke got home and finished his chores.''

"Yes, I heard all about it from Adam." Nell chuckled. "And that's one of the reasons I'm calling. It seems luck is with us again. I hate to keep wishing illnesses on people, but now Luke and Greg have come down with that bad flu that's going around this year. Luke took Scott to the doctor last night and found out it was more than just a virus. Adam is the only one still on his feet, and he's going crazy trying to take care of everybody else."

"Poor boy. I'll fix some soup and take it over to them. Maybe I can even spend the night and—" Betty stopped and a knowing smile spread across her face. "Oh...it's too bad, but I just remembered that I've got something *very* important to do tomorrow, so I couldn't possibly go over there and take care of Luke and the boys. But Darcy could."

"Darcy could what?"

Betty almost dropped the phone as Darcy walked into the kitchen unexpectedly. "Uh...I'm talking to Nell and she's really worried about Greg and Scott."

Darcy got a glass out of the cabinet, walked to the refrigerator and poured a glass of orange juice. "Oh, why?"

"Because they've both got the flu, too. Poor little Adam's trying hard, but he can't handle all those sick people and the chores."

"What's his father doing?"

"Oh, I forgot to mention that he's sick, too. They're all in bed."

"So what am I supposed to do about it?" Darcy asked with growing suspicion.

"I'm going to make them some soup, but they need someone to handle things. Adam has to go to school during the day, so he can't stay up all night with the patients."

"But I can?" Darcy asked wryly.

"How sweet of you to volunteer," Betty declared, then spoke into the telephone receiver. "Darcy just offered to stay with the boys and help them." She listened for a moment, then said to Darcy, "Nell wanted to tell you how much she appreciates your offer. She has so much to worry about with her sister and all, that she doesn't need to be worrying about the boys, too. Especially since she's hundreds of miles away. And I'd do it, but I've already promised to drive to Omaha with your father tomorrow to look at a new tractor."

Darcy nodded. There was a perceptive gleam in her eyes. "Why do I feel this is a setup?"

"I don't know what you mean." Betty tried to look innocent. "They're really sick. We wouldn't lie about that. Would we, Nell?"

Darcy's smile was good-natured. She knew when she was outnumbered. "Okay, but tell Nell I don't guarantee there'll be any survivors. Nursing is not one of my skills. And neither is patience." Darcy rinsed out her glass and left it in the sink. "I guess I'd better go pack a few things. I'll bet Luke will be thrilled to have me holding his head while he's losing his dinner."

Betty waited until her daughter was out of the room and up the stairs before adding to Nell, "I hope this doesn't backfire on us. You know how men are when they're sick."

"Yes, Luke's a bigger baby than Scott," Nell confirmed. "This is definitely a trial by fire. By the time Darcy leaves, she'll either love them or hate them."

"WHAT ARE YOU doing here?"

The question was the same, but the attitude was different. While before he had been suspicious and certainly not welcoming, this time he was vague and unfocused as if he couldn't believe his own eyes.

"What are you doing out of bed?" Darcy tossed her coat across the chair and dropped her purse on the kitchen table. "You look like—"

"Don't say it," Luke moaned. "If I look even half as bad as I feel, then it's definitely not a word I want my kids to hear."

He was leaning heavily against the counter and offered no resistance as Darcy took the bottle of cough syrup from his hand. "Is this for you or one of the other sick men in this house?"

"Who's sick? I've just got a little cold." As if for emphasis, he sneezed, but the effort almost made him fall.

Darcy caught him by the arm and began propelling him toward the stairs. "Where's your bedroom?"

"Feeling frisky, are we?" he managed to ask.

"I make it a policy never to take advantage of an unconscious man, which is what you're going to be if we don't get your fever down." She could feel the heat of his body, a very different heat than was generated by their embraces. And a new, odd emotion touched her. This man needed her... not forever, but at the moment, he needed her very much. Darcy couldn't remember ever having actually been *needed* by anyone in her life.

Oh sure, there were people depending on her to show up for work each day, to pay her house and car payments on time, even to present the news as honestly and professionally as possible. But no one would actually be in trouble if she didn't do what was expected of her.

"Dad, where's my medicine?" Greg called from the living-room couch where he was reclining, covered with blankets.

"I want some orange juice." Scott's voice drifted down the stairs, followed by a fit of coughing.

"I'm on my way," Luke called, but he was leaning against Darcy so limply that she was staggering under his weight.

Yes, Darcy was definitely needed in this house.

After tucking him, fully clothed, into his bed, Darcy rummaged through the medicine cabinet until she found a thermometer. Leaving it stuck under Luke's tongue, she stopped off at Scott's room.

"How're you today?" she asked, knowing by his flushed coloring that his fever had returned.

"I thought this would be gone today," Scott whined. "I don't like being sick."

"Did you say you wanted some orange juice?"

"Yes, I'm so thirsty."

"Well, I'm not sure orange juice will be good for your stomach, but a doctor once told me that if we crave something, then our body needs it." She patted Scott's cheek. "I'll be back in a minute. Okay?"

He nodded and relaxed against his pillow.

Darcy went back to Luke's room and took the thermometer out of his mouth.

"It's about time," he grumbled. "I was beginning to think you'd forgotten me."

"Now don't start getting cranky. I can handle coughs, fever and even a little whining. But I won't tolerate crankiness."

"That's not a very good attitude for a nurse."

"I'm not a nurse, I'm a commentator."

He chuckled. "That reminds me of a joke about a family of taters who—"

"Oh, and I forgot to add that I hate dumb jokes."

"This is a house full of dumb jokes."

Darcy's eyebrows lifted quizzically. "I couldn't have phrased it better myself."

Luke's frown was confused as he tried to sit up. "That didn't turn out like I meant it."

"Never mind." Darcy pushed him back down. "You've got a temperature of one hundred and three. Take off your pants and put on your pajamas while I go downstairs and get some medicine and orange juice for all of you."

"Take off my pants, huh?" he mumbled with a loose grin.

"Men!" Darcy declared as she wheeled around and headed back to Scott's room. "They have a one-track mind, even when they're sick."

After checking Scott's temperature, which was hovering at just over one hundred degrees, Darcy cleaned the thermometer, tucked it into its case and put it into her pants pocket. She suspected she would be using the fragile instrument often during the next few hours.

When she went to check on Greg in the living room, she was greeted by a less than friendly glare. But his fevered eyes told her he was in no condition to challenge her authority. Meekly he accepted the thermometer, shuddering at the mild alcohol taste that lingered on the glass from when Darcy had sterilized it.

"Ith Gwanma comin' home to tek cur of uth?" he asked, his words garbled by the thermometer.

"I'm pretty good with dialects, but you've got me with that one," Darcy answered.

Greg waited until she removed the instrument and was trying to read the numbers above the line of mercury. "Is Grandma coming home to take care of us?" he repeated.

"No, there's no reason for her to leave your aunt alone. You guys will be up and around in a few days."

"I've got to go to school tomorrow. I'm supposed to go to the hobby shop with Dave."

"I think you'll have to plan that trip for another day," Darcy stated as she shook the mercury back down. "Your temperature is almost as high as your father's. Even if you're feeling better, I doubt that Dave would appreciate breathing your germs."

Greg heaved an annoyed sigh and sunk deeper into the cushions.

"Is there anything I can get you? Do you want some soup or something?"

"Nah, just leave me alone."

Darcy tried not to let his attitude bother her. Even though he was sixteen, he was still just a kid. And he probably would have acted the same way to any strange woman who appeared to be horning in on his family. She knew it was useless to try to explain that she had no intention of joining his family, so she remained silent.

However, she returned a couple of minutes later with some cold tablets, a glass of water and a pot in case his stomach rebelled. He swallowed the dosage without comment, then turned his back to her as he studied the television with more intensity than a sitcom repeat deserved.

She shook off his rudeness and returned upstairs to take Scott his medicine and a glass of orange juice as she had promised. A quick visit to Luke's room confirmed that he was already asleep. She roused him enough to force a couple of tablets down with a drink of water. Then after he lay back down, she straightened his blanket and turned off his bedside lamp. For just a moment, she stood, glancing around the room in the semidarkness.

Apparently, Nell's feminine influence didn't extend into Luke's room. A compound bow and a quiver of arrows hung from a rack on one wall while a gun cabinet, filled with rifles, dominated the opposite wall. There were a couple of framed prints of Indians and several sets of deer antlers mounted on plaques. It was definitely a man's room. She doubted there would be enough drawer or closet space to accommodate a woman's clothes ... certainly not hers.

Not that it mattered, of course. Her clothes would never hang in Luke's closet.

Adam was in the kitchen when she returned downstairs. She automatically felt his forehead, checking for fever, but he was blessedly cool.

"So, how have you escaped this plague?" she asked, flashing him a relieved smile.

"Grandma says I'm too mean for germs to survive," Adam retorted, but his grin showed he hadn't been insulted. Instead, it was almost as if he was proud of his reputation.

"Did you finish the chores? I can help you if you'll show me what to do."

"Nah, there's nothing left to do tonight. All I had to do was check their water, give them some food and lock them in for the night."

"Lock them in? Why? Do they try to sneak into town at night?" she teased.

Adam snorted. "Town is the last place they'd try to get to. That's where the processing plant is."

"You have a good point."

"I have to lock the doors to keep dogs and wild animals out of the barns. The turkeys don't need to have their rest disturbed."

Darcy nodded. "I can certainly understand that. There are few animals who need their beauty sleep more than turkeys do."

An appreciative twinkle finally touched his blue eyes, eyes that were very different from his father's.

Another contribution of Luke's long-lost beloved wife, no doubt.

"So, what do you want for dinner?" Darcy steered her thoughts toward a new topic. "Not that you have all that much of a selection since I can't cook anything complicated. How about some soup or a sandwich?"

"Okay. I like chicken noodle, the fat kind, but without the mushrooms."

Darcy surveyed the contents of the pantry, trying to decide which of the soup cans contained fat noodles. Adam must have sensed her confusion because he walked over and selected one of the cans.

"This is it," he announced. "There's enough for two people if you want some, too. And I'll make some nachos."

It wasn't the sort of dinner she was accustomed to, but it was warm and filling. After the meal, she checked again on her patients, all of whom were fitfully asleep, then returned to the kitchen.

"Do you have any homework?"

"Not much. I can do it tomorrow in study hall," Adam answered, then slid Darcy a measuring look. "That is, unless I stay home from school tomorrow. I could help out around here and do my homework later."

"No, you'd better go to school. Who knows whether or not those germs will break through your defenses and make you miss a few days of classes later." Darcy loaded the dishes into the dishwasher. "I think you'd better get that homework done tonight. Bring it in here and I'll help you."

Adam groaned, but he obeyed. He dropped his book bag on the table, zipped it open and pulled out his books and some paper. "Do you think we could play a game after we get through with this?"

"I suppose we could if you finish early enough. What time do you usually go to bed?"

Adam didn't miss a beat as he answered, "Eleven o'clock."

Darcy gave him a knowing look. "Nine o'clock?"

"Ten-thirty."

"Okay, we'll compromise. Ten o'clock, but you have to go straight to bed."

He nodded eagerly and opened his book. "Do you know anything about geography?"

"It's my specialty. I hated it when I was in school, but after I decided to become a newscaster, I knew I'd better learn it." She flipped through his book until she found a map of the world. "Here, I'll show you all the places I've been."

The time passed quickly. Adam was genuinely interested in hearing of her experiences around the world. He was very bright, quickly picking up on the details and asking lots of questions. To award his achievement they played his favorite board game after he finished his homework.

Finally, Darcy glanced at her watch. "It's five minutes until ten. Go brush your teeth and jump into bed. I've got to make another round with the thermometer and medicine."

Adam repacked his books into his bag and picked up his game.

"Good night, Adam. See you in the morning."

"Uh...do you think you could...maybe..." He hesitated. "I mean, if you want to, you could tuck me in."

A strange feeling gripped Darcy's heart. She looked at Adam and smiled. Beneath his prickly, barely teen-aged exterior, he was a sweet, vulnerable child. One minute he could be picking mercilessly on his younger brother and the next be discussing the presidential election like an adult and handling a man's chores. Yes, she found herself growing to like Adam as much as she already liked Scott.

"Sure, I'll tuck you in," she said, and was touched by the obvious relief that crossed his features. He must have been worried she would say no, or worse, laugh at him. "You run along. I'll be up there in a minute."

She listened to his feet on the stairs, followed by the sound of running water as he rushed through the task of brushing his teeth. It was an odd feeling, this one-on-one communication. She wasn't used to sharing her life or her space with another human on a personal level. Ever since she left her parents' home, she had been alone. And when she talked to the viewers, there was always that comforting fourth wall between her and them.

And that was the way she liked it. Sooner or later these kids would begin to get on her nerves. No, it wasn't wise of her to get too close to them. They might get their hopes up that she would be sticking around. She didn't want to hurt them. They'd already lost their mother. They didn't need to suffer through another loss.

But she couldn't leave yet. They needed her.

# Chapter Nine

The sun sneaked through the crack between the draperies and inched its way across the floor and up on the bed, finally landing a direct shot into Luke's eyes. He fought against wakening, hugging the warm, dark shroud of sleep. Drifting in and out of awareness, he felt something soft press against his forehead, gently feathering through his hair. A sweet scent drifted into his nostrils, a fragrance as fresh and independent as the woman who wore it.

"Darcy," he whispered hoarsely through the rawness of his throat. Slowly, he forced his eyes open.

It took him a few seconds to focus on each item in his room as his gaze searched for her. But he was alone. He must have been dreaming. How odd that it would be about Darcy.

Luke rubbed his eyes. They felt like they had a pound of sand in each one. And his mouth tasted like something had died in it. He ran his tongue along his teeth. He definitely needed to get to his toothbrush as soon as possible. And about a gallon of mouthwash wouldn't hurt, either.

He glanced at the clock and was amazed to see it was almost noon. Why had he slept so late? What day was it? Didn't the kids have school? Even if it was Saturday, he had to finish loading barn five into his truck and take them to market.

Tossing back the covers he started to sit up, but the room began spinning around him. His legs felt strangely shaky, much too weak for him to stand. In fact, his whole body was trembling and he felt a cold sweat wash over him.

His confusion increased. Brief flashes of memories began pushing into his consciousness. He had been working in the barn when the dizziness struck. He knew he had been pushing himself lately, spending long hours trying to get the turkeys to the processing plant on time. It was promising to be his best season yet.

But all of a sudden it had hit him. He felt exhausted. Every muscle in his body ached and his head was pounding. Even lifting the little red flag he used to herd the turkeys was too much of an effort.

He remembered calling Adam to come take over with the turkeys. Luke had sat outside, enjoying the cool November air until the truck was loaded. Then, somehow, he had managed to drive safely to the processor and back. At least he assumed he had; he didn't remember anything about the trip.

The next thing he recalled was trying to give Scott his medicine and take care of Greg when all the while Luke could barely summon the energy to breathe. There wasn't a part of his body that didn't hurt. Then he looked up and Darcy had been there.

Darcy. She was the last person he had expected to see at that moment...and the one person he had wanted most. She'd taken over, pushing him into bed, sticking a thermometer halfway down his throat, then forcing him to swallow some pills.

His memory from there was sketchy. There were trips to the bathroom and glasses of liquid and more medicine poured into him. But he must have slept for over twelve hours.

Again, he tried to stand and was met with an unsteady success as long as he held on to something. Dressed only in a pair of white briefs and a T-shirt, he decided he'd better put on a robe at the very least. Moving slowly, he crossed to the bathroom, brushed his teeth and pulled on the old terry cloth robe Ellen had given him for Christmas seven years ago.

He stopped at Scott's room, but found his son's bed empty, which only multiplied his feelings of guilt. Luke should have been the one to take care of his son, not a neighbor. The sound of voices downstairs drew him even though he had to hold on to the banisters and take his descent slow.

"That's mine. You owe me one hundred fifty dollars," Adam declared.

"That's the second time I've landed on that," Greg grumbled. "But you're getting close to my greens. With the hotels on them, it's going to cost you more than twelve hundred dollars."

There was the sound of paper shuffling, then the tumble of dice across the cardboard.

"Twelve!" Adam shouted. "I landed on Chance and missed all your stupid greens."

Luke finally reached the doorway and watched, unobserved, for a few seconds as Scott played his turn. He frowned as he stopped moving his piece forward.

"I own Tennessee Avenue." Adam checked his card. "With three houses, you owe me five hundred fifty dollars. I guess you lost the game."

Scott counted his money, but Luke could tell by the little boy's expression of desperation that he didn't have enough. Suddenly, a five-hundred-dollar bill fell into Scott's lap, dropped by Darcy under the table where the other two boys couldn't see. Scott's gaze fell to the money and he smiled.

"No problem," he stated as he added a fifty-dollar bill to the five hundred and passed them to Greg.

"Where'd you get that? You're almost broke."

"It was in my lap." Scott's innocent look matched Darcy's as she picked up the dice and rolled them.

"Dad!" Adam called, noticing Luke at last. "Do you want to play?"

The game halted as everyone turned to look at Luke.

"No, I'll just watch. How's everyone feeling?"

"Fine," Scott answered.

"Better," Greg added.

"I have a headache," Adam stated.

Everyone transferred their attention to him as Greg and Scott scooted their chairs away. Darcy stood and walked to Adam.

"You do look a little flushed." She whipped the thermometer case out of the pocket of her bulky sweater, took out the glass tube and stuck it in Adam's mouth.

"You handle that like a pro." Luke chuckled.

"I've had enough practice for the past three days." She pulled a chair over to him. "You'd better sit down. You don't look like you've gotten your land legs back yet."

He *was* feeling shaky, so he sat without offering an objection. "Three days?"

"Yes, Rip Van Winkle. I've been here for three days while you slept."

Luke straightened, but groaned as his aching muscles protested. "I've been asleep for three days? That isn't possible. Yesterday was Wednesday and I took Mom to Des Moines. . . ."

"Yesterday was Friday," Darcy corrected. She took the thermometer out of Adam's mouth and shifted it between her forefinger and thumb until she could see the mercury. "One hundred. Congratulations, young man. Your germs are meaner than you thought. Off to bed."

"I feel okay," Adam protested. "I want to finish the game."

"We'll play again when you get well," Darcy stated firmly. "If you go to bed now, maybe it won't hit you as hard as it did your dad and Scott."

"I was sick only two days." Greg sounded pleased, as if he'd had some sort of control of his illness.

Luke was still trying to accept that he'd been in bed for three days. How had things gone on without him? What about the farm? "Are the turkeys all right?"

Darcy wiped the thermometer with alcohol and inserted it into Luke's open mouth. "Well, I haven't taken any of their temperatures, and I think if a flu bug got anywhere near them, they'd have eaten it. I've never seen any creatures eat like those birds do."

"They don't have much else to think about, you know," Greg pointed out.

Luke jerked the thermometer out of his mouth. "Who fed and watered them?" he asked in a strained voice. He was having trouble getting a straight answer from anyone about anything.

"Adam did. I wasn't sure he could handle it, but he did a great job," Darcy said, patting Adam's shoulder.

"Darcy helped," Adam added.

"But you had to tell me everything to do," Darcy hurried to add. She and Adam exchanged a companionable smile. "Now, go change into your pajamas and get into bed. I'll bring you a glass of juice and your medicine. And make sure your gerbil and snake have water and food before you collapse. I absolutely draw the line at taking care of them."

Adam grumbled, but he obeyed. "I would have to get sick on a Saturday."

Darcy took Luke's hand and guided the thermometer back into his mouth, then helped the other boys put up the Monopoly game. "We were going to have pizza for dinner. Do you think you're ready for that?"

Luke shook his head. His illness hadn't started off with an upset stomach like Scott's had, but he still didn't think he was ready for something spicy so soon.

"I'll make you some more soup." She opened the pantry and sorted through the cans. "Is chunky vegetable beef okay? We've gone through a lot of soup. I haven't had a chance to get to the store since Thursday evening.''

Luke took the thermometer out of his mouth again. "You went grocery shopping?"

"Don't sound so shocked. I buy groceries all the time. I'm not a total incompetent in the kitchen. I just don't cook."

"What else is there to do in a kitchen?" Luke asked, immediately regretting the question when he saw the eloquent arch of her eyebrow.

"Never mind," he continued. "I don't want to know what you do in your kitchen."

"I do, Daddy," Scott chirped.

"Why don't you go play with Joe and Linda?" Darcy suggested. "They've really been missing you."

"Can I?" Scott's eyes brightened. "Do you think I'm well enough."

"Sure. You've passed the Carson thermometer test," Darcy said. "But bundle up. We're supposed to get some snow tonight and the wind might pick up at any time."

"Snow? Tonight?" Luke echoed, feeling as if he truly were Rip Van Winkle. He fell asleep and when he woke up the whole world had changed. With the exception of Greg who had left to go to his bedroom and still seemed to be determined to keep a little distance between him and Darcy, the kids were getting along with her as if she was an old family friend. The turkeys had been taken care of and the weather was taking a drastic turn for the worse. What more had happened while he slept?

Scott ran for the hall closet while Darcy returned to Luke.

"If you don't leave that thing in your mouth longer, I'll never get an accurate reading of your temperature," she reprimanded.

He put the thermometer back under his tongue, then promptly pulled it out again. "But I need to get out there and check on the turkeys. If we have a snowstorm..."

She gave him a severe look that made him return the glass instrument to his mouth.

"First we find out if you're getting well," she informed him. "Then we'll decide who's going to do the chores."

Scott ran through the kitchen, pausing briefly for an inspection by Darcy before going outside to play with his pets.

While Luke impatiently waited for a minute to pass, she gave him a quick rundown on Greg and Scott's illnesses and Adam's helpfulness. Luke started to point out that cooperation was not a common trait of Adam's, but he was so astounded at his son's behavior that he remained quiet. Besides, he knew Darcy would give him another of those looks if he touched the thermometer again.

"And your mother called last night," Darcy continued as she opened the can of soup. "She said your aunt Louise is doing pretty well, and that she'll try to call you tomorrow after church to see how everyone is."

Luke's gaze focused on the provocative curve of Darcy's behind as she bent to get a saucepan out of the cabinet. A pair of skin-tight white stirrup pants displayed her long beautiful legs and rounded backside to their best advantage. Her feet were bare, and he noticed that her toenails were painted a bright coral red that almost exactly matched the bulky sweater.

She straightened, and Luke was disappointed when the long, loose hem of the sweater fell back to her thighs. He knew he must be on the road to recovery as his gaze moved over the bulky knit to the tempting mounds of her breasts. The material looked so soft . . . but he suspected it was rough compared to the silkiness of her skin beneath it.

As soon as the soup was cooking, Darcy crossed to Luke and removed the thermometer. While she studied it, he studied her. Her fragrance surrounded him, pulling him to his feet. She looked up, startled, meeting his eyes over the thermometer.

There was a questioning quiver in her voice as she informed him, "Ninety-eight point six. You're back to normal."

"No more germs?"

"I guess not."

"I don't know how to thank you for . . . well, everything."

She shook her head, sending her rich, auburn hair tumbling over her shoulders. "It was the neighborly thing to do."

"Yes, but technically, you're not my neighbor."

"No, but I'd like to think we'll be friends even after I go back to the West Coast."

He leaned his head toward her. "I'm not sure if I want to be your friend."

"Oh?" she asked.

He hooked his finger under her chin and lifted her head. "I've never made love to a friend."

"My, we *are* feeling better, aren't we?" Her lovely blue eyes twinkled.

"We could feel better."

"Oh?" she repeated a little breathlessly.

"I've missed you."

"I've been right here."

"No, I mean I've missed holding you in my arms and kissing you," he whispered against her lips. "What magic spell did you cast on me that makes me dream about you when I'm asleep and think about you when I'm awake?"

"I'm a newscaster, not a spellcaster."

His lips moved over hers, touching, nibbling, teasing, but not quite kissing . . . yet. "Here's a news flash for you. I'm not completely well. I've got a pain . . . way down deep . . . that only you can make feel better."

"Now I'm feeling a little dizzy," she murmured against his lips.

"Then let me take your temperature," Luke offered.

"With the thermometer?"

"No," he breathed before he let his hands move down the back of her sweater until they cupped the fullness of her buttocks and pulled her against him.

Her arms circled his neck. No longer able to keep from kissing her, he pressed his mouth against hers. Soft. Her lips were soft. Her breasts, flattened against his chest, were soft. Her hair was even softer than her sweater. His hands slipped under the hem to the soft, warm skin of her back.

"Luke, don't..." Darcy whispered. "Your boys could walk in. They're not ready for this."

Luke knew she was right. He hated it, but this was not the time or the place. But would there ever be a right time or place? "How about you?" he couldn't resist asking before he let her go. "Are you ready for this?"

She didn't answer, but the sexy, flirtatious smile said it all.

"Maybe later when they're all asleep we can finish this... discussion," he suggested.

"Are they *ever* all asleep?" she asked. "It seems like someone is always awake and needing something."

The back door opened and they had only a couple of seconds to separate and try to appear casual by the time Scott bounced back into the room. Luke sat at the table and Darcy brought him a bowl of soup with all the familiarity of a family at dinnertime.

"They were sure glad to see me." Scott brushed the leaves off his clothes. He explained cheerfully, "Joe knocked me over and sat on me. Then Linda untied my shoestrings."

"Do you want any soup?" Darcy asked him, helping him take off his coat.

He nodded and walked toward the sink to wash his hands. "What happened to your face?" Scott asked, peering up at her. "It's all red. Are you getting the fever?"

Darcy and Luke exchanged glances over the boy's head. Luke's hand stroked his two-day stubble, knowing that was why her face seemed flushed.

"No, I don't think so," she answered as she turned away and poured the contents of the pan into a bowl, then placed it on the table. "It must be from the steam off the soup."

"Everybody else has had the fever in our house," Scott continued. "When you get it, you can sleep in Daddy's room and he'll take care of you like you took care of us."

Behind Scott, Luke nodded enthusiastically and Darcy gave him a teasing smile.

"I doubt that I'll get sick. You see, I travel a lot in my job so I have to keep up-to-date with my shots, including flu shots."

"That's too bad. I was hoping to repay you... somehow," Luke told her, telegraphing with his eyes just what it was he had in mind.

"Uh... I'd better get that juice up to Adam. I'll bet he's wondering what happened."

Luke could certainly understand that sentiment... he was wondering what was happening, too. He watched her pour the juice, gather the medicine and a spoon and walk out of the room. Boy, that woman knew how to walk. And kiss. And...?

He didn't want to think about how she might have gotten her experience. For a surprisingly selfish reason, he wanted her to be his alone. He would never have believed it, but she could fit into his life. Adam and Scott adored her, and even Greg was thawing. He wished she had no past. Even more, he wished there was some possibility that he would be her future.

He had vowed when he first met her that he'd never ask her to stay. And he remained firm with that resolve. If she decided to stay, it would have to be her own decision, not because he had gotten down on his knees and begged her.

However, it wouldn't be totally unfair to pull out all the stops and try to convince her that life with him and his family on a turkey farm in Iowa was much more desirable than life alone in Los Angeles. He would woo her and win her love. When it came time to go back, she wouldn't be able to say goodbye.

He felt much stronger after he finished his soup, strong enough to begin his campaign of capturing her heart.

"Dad, is Darcy going to stay here with us while Grandma's gone?" Scott asked.

"No, she only stayed here because I was too sick to take care of you guys," Luke explained. "But I'm going to try to get her to spend a lot of time with us during the next two weeks. Would you like that?"

"Yeah, Darcy's the prettiest, nicest girl I've ever met," Scott announced positively.

And Luke couldn't have agreed more.

"I'm going to go check on the turkeys. Want to go with me?"

"Aren't you going to put on some pants?"

Luke looked down at his bare legs. It was so unusual for him to be sitting in his kitchen in the middle of the day while still wearing little more than a bathrobe that he'd forgotten how awful he must look. If he was going to make any sort of a *positive* impression on Darcy, he'd better improve the packaging. "Yeah, I guess I'd better get some pants before I go outside. Then I'm going to hit the shower. Make sure Darcy doesn't leave until I get through."

He was back from the turkey barns and in the kitchen less than an hour later, showered, shaved and fully dressed for the first time in two days. Darcy was standing at the sink, rinsing Scott's bowl. Part of a large pizza, still in the delivery box, was on the table while Greg sat in front of it, his plate full.

"Sure you don't want any pizza?" she asked Luke.

"I'm feeling better, but not that good."

She turned off the water, wiped her hands and walked toward the table where she had left her overnight bag, coat and purse. "I guess it's safe for me to leave now. I think you're all going to survive."

Luke stepped forward quickly. "Don't go yet. I mean, I was wondering if you'd ride into town with me and pick up a few more groceries."

"Too weak to drive?" she taunted, not the least bit fooled by his excuse to get them away from the house.

"Too weak to shop," he answered.

"I want to go," Scott declared.

"No, you're going to stay here and help Greg with the chores." Luke turned to his oldest son and asked, "Would you do the feeding this afternoon?"

Greg, too, knew exactly what was going on, and it was evident from his expression that he didn't approve. But he didn't voice his objections. Instead, he nodded, "Sure, I guess so."

Luke asked, "Did you have any plans tonight?"

"Nah, Dave, Brian and Paul all have the flu."

"So, Darcy, will you go with me to the grocery store? I'll even buy you dinner later."

"As pathetic as it may be, that's the best offer I've gotten all week."

As they walked toward the back door, Greg asked, "What time will you be home?"

The irony of the role reversal wasn't lost on Luke. "I'm not sure, but don't wait up."

"It takes that long to shop for groceries?"

Luke gave Greg a warning look. "I haven't shopped in a while. Don't worry about it."

Luke took Darcy's arm and was almost outside when he heard Greg call, "Don't forget your seat belts."

Darcy settled onto the plush velour seats and waited until Luke had backed the car out of his garage and was driving down the county road before she commented, "You and Greg were having a private conversation, weren't you?"

"Greg thinks he's all grown-up and knows everything. I suppose I was the same way when I was sixteen."

"Weren't we all," Darcy agreed.

"He and I have always gotten along so well," Luke mused. "But lately...we just seem to be on different planets."

"I think that's a teenage symptom, too."

"Lord, I hope we both live through it." He glanced over and flashed her a very personal smile. "Let's stop talking about the boys. I'm sure you've just about overdosed on instant motherhood this week."

She thought about the almost sleepless night on Thursday when she'd been up and down with Scott, Greg and Luke, watching their temperatures rise and fall, giving them medicine, helping them get comfortable. There had been the meals, however simple and often delivered by Pizza Hut, and the dishes. She'd even spent some time getting to know the turkeys better.

But all in all, she was able to answer honestly, "It wasn't so bad. I'm not sure I could handle it on a regular basis, but it helped pass the time."

She noticed his hands tightened on the wheel, then relaxed. "Just marking time," he remarked.

"It was either coming here or staying in the public eye in L.A." She looked out at the gently rolling farmland they were passing, knowing they could drive for miles without seeing a single person. That was certainly not the case where she lived.

"So your decision had nothing to do with coming home for the holidays?"

She turned back to face him. "I didn't think it did when I first made the decision. Sure, I wanted to see Mother and Dad. But, other than the human-interest stories, increased crime rate and the shopping, the holidays haven't meant much to me for the past few years. I haven't eaten turkey at Thanksgiving or decorated a tree for eight or nine years."

Luke gave a dramatic gasp. "So you're the one who hasn't been buying a turkey for Thanksgiving! I have a son who'll be going to college in a couple of years."

"Sorry," she said and held up her hand as she pledged, "I promise I'll buy one from now on. Even if I donate it to a needy family. I wouldn't want your kids to miss out on a college degree just because of me."

"They really like you, you know." His comment was casual.

"And I really like them. They're nice kids. They don't take after you, do they?"

He pretended to be insulted. "Thanks a lot."

"No, I didn't mean their personalities. I meant their looks. I saw a picture of your wife in the living room." Darcy dropped her gaze to her hands that were folded in her lap. "She was very pretty."

"Yes, she was. She and I were high school sweethearts. As soon as we graduated, she got a job and helped put me through college." He was silent for a moment as if savoring a favorite thought from the past. "We planned on living the American dream with two children, a house in the city and a yearly vacation to Hawaii or Europe. Maybe both."

"But Scott came along and made it three kids," Darcy pointed out.

"He was unexpected, but certainly not unwanted. He rounded out the family, making it even better than before. Oh sure, we had disagreements, but overall, we were happy." He shrugged. "And then it happened. One brief moment... and everything changed. Ellen was driving home from a visit with her mother. It was icy and Ellen's car slid in front of a truck. Scott was with her, but he was strapped into his car seat and wasn't hurt. But Ellen wasn't wearing a seat belt." He heaved a heavy, pained sigh. "She was thrown from the car... through the windshield."

"I'm so sorry," Darcy said, reaching out to place a comforting hand on his arm. "It's always a terrible thing to lose a loved one in a car accident, but when there're small children involved, it's even worse."

He pulled into the grocery store parking lot and turned off the engine. Facing Darcy, he managed a cheerful smile. "Boy, do I know how to cramp an evening. I said I wasn't going to talk about the boys anymore, and what do I talk about instead...?"

"I'm glad you told me," Darcy assured him. "I wanted to know, but I hated to ask. I've never really been in love, so I can't imagine how awful it would be." She knew the hurt would be there forever. How could any woman ever hope to fit into such a huge void?

Oh sure, sooner or later Luke would remarry. But would he ever be able to love his new wife as much as he had loved Ellen? Wouldn't any new woman be a poor substitute for the woman with whom he had shared so much?

Darcy had always been confident of her skills, so confident that she was rarely nervous in job interviews. But she knew she would be quaking in her boots if she truly cared for Luke enough to want to become a permanent part of his family. Any woman, even one with far more domestic talents than Darcy, would have a rough time trying to be a substitute wife and mother.

It would be like replacing Walter Cronkite. People may try, but no one could ever really take his place.

Thank goodness Darcy didn't have the time or inclination to fall in love with Luke. She had never liked being a backup.

# Chapter Ten

"You have to squeeze it." Darcy demonstrated. "It might look good on the outside, but you want the inside to be full and hard."

There was a sexy gleam in his eyes as he followed her lead. "Full and hard is *always* better."

"Luke! I'm talking about lettuce."

The twinkle turned mischievous. "So am I. What else would I be talking about?"

"I'd hate to guess," Darcy commented wryly.

He handed her the head of lettuce he'd been testing. "How's this one?"

She gave it a perfunctory squeeze. "It's fine. Now do you need a lesson in oranges?"

"I thought you didn't know anything about cooking?"

"I didn't say I didn't *know* anything. I just said I *couldn't* cook. It's not like riding a bicycle."

"You lost me there."

She continued the conversation as they walked along together with Luke pushing the basket. "My mother insisted that I learn how to cook. And I wasn't a total failure. But once I moved away from home and began to prepare meals for myself, I gradually made them simpler and simpler. Now I have so little time that I usually eat most of my meals out or toss together a salad or throw a frozen dinner into the microwave. There are some pretty good frozen meals now, not like when I was a kid."

"So what does that have to do with a bicycle?"

"You know how they say you never forget how to ride a bicycle? I found my old one in the barn the other day and did a few laps around the house, and I hadn't touched a bicycle in fifteen years. But the same principle doesn't hold true with cooking. Every once in a while I get the urge to put a meal together, but I've forgotten all the little tricks. Things don't turn out right." She deftly selected some oranges and twisted a fastener on top of the plastic bag. "Don't they have any paper bags here? Don't they know that plastic is forever?"

"This is Iowa. We live with natural every day, so occasional plastic is a luxury." He took the bag from her and put it into the basket. "So I guess because you live in California, you're an expert on fruit and nuts?"

She gave him a sharp glance. "Have you ever been to California?"

He shook his head. "No."

"It's a nice place. Somewhere in the state there are mountains, oceans, deserts, rich farmland and everything in between. You've never seen fruit as big or as delicious. I've got some orange and lemon and even two avocado trees in my backyard."

"All right, I concede. You're the expert."

"You should bring the kids out next summer. They'd love Disneyland."

The look they exchanged was solemn, almost sad. Darcy was instantly sorry she'd mentioned it because it reminded them of the inevitable. Soon she would be back in L.A. and he would still be here.

A half hour later they had explored every aisle, checked out and loaded the bags into the car. They drove to the nicest restaurant in town and lingered over the delicious Italian food.

"Are you sure you shouldn't get back to the boys?" Darcy asked, not wanting the evening to end early, but not wanting to think she was keeping him from his fatherly duties.

"No, they're fine. I called home while you were in the ladies' room and Greg said Adam's temperature was down and Scott was already in bed." He leaned back in his chair. "Even parents need a night out every once in a while."

"*Especially* parents," Darcy corrected.

"Don't you ever want to marry and have kids of your own?" Luke studied her over the rim of his wine glass.

A month ago she would have said, "Probably not." But today, she wasn't so quick to dismiss the possibility. She knew motherhood wasn't all roses. But spending time with Luke's kids had made her think about what her own might be like. She and Adam had had some interesting discussions, and how could she ignore the pleasure of Scott's arms around her neck?

"I'm not sure a marriage would fit into my lifestyle, but I might think about having a child in a couple of years."

He tried not to register his disapproval, but it was evident in his eyes. "It's not easy raising kids as a single parent."

"But people do it all the time."

"That's usually out of necessity instead of choice."

"I just don't know if I have enough to give a marriage. It takes work and commitment."

"So does parenthood."

Darcy sighed. "That's what I'll have to decide. Perhaps I'll get a chance to be an anchor on national news or my own current events show. Then I'd have the security and a more regular schedule so I would have something to offer a child."

His expression was speculative and totally unconvinced.

"Maybe it's difficult for you to understand how important my work is to me."

"No, I've met lots of of people who loved their work . . . more than anything else in their lives," Luke answered. "I've seen both sides, and, for me at least, there is more to life than work. I could have kept my practice and spent twelve hours a day fixing teeth and building my bank balance. But my kids were growing up without me. I wanted them to learn the good, honest values of the heartland instead of survival of the fittest in the city."

"So that worked for you and your kids, and my lifestyle is working for me," Darcy pointed out.

Luke looked as if he wanted to say something else on the subject, but he reached into his pocket and withdrew his wallet. He paid the check and they left the restaurant.

The forecast of snow had finally come true. Already a light powdering covered the ground and the vehicles in the parking lot, and it was continuing to fall from the sky in a light but steady shower. The roads weren't slick, but visibility was poor, so Luke had to pay close attention to his driving.

When they were safely parked in his garage, Darcy tilted her head and remarked, "That was a much more comfortable ride than the last time you and I drove together."

"I was making a point."

"Yes, and I believe that point was sticking through the seat."

"Sorry about that. I could tell you that I drove the truck because Mom needed the car to take the boys to the fair, but you would know that wasn't the whole truth. I was trying to make you uncomfortable." He gave her a sheepish grin. "Because *I* was uncomfortable."

"I didn't want to be there any more than you did," she reminded him.

"And now?" He turned to face her, carefully studying her expression.

Her voice was soft as she answered, "I've always loved county fairs. But this year's was the best yet."

He leaned across the space that separated them and surprised her with a kiss. "To keep from destroying what little pride I have left, I will assume it was because of my stimulating company."

"It certainly wasn't because of the transportation," Darcy retorted, refusing to let the conversation get too serious. She could handle her emotions as long as she kept things light.

She helped Luke carry the groceries into the quiet house, then said, "Thanks for dinner. I guess I'd better get on home. It'll be nice to sleep in my old bed, even if it's not my *real* bed."

"You mean you've been sleeping here?" Luke was obviously surprised.

"You were in no condition to watch the boys."

"Where did you sleep?"

"In Nell's room. I hope she won't mind. It was either that or the top bunk of Scott's bed." She reached for her lower back and groaned. "I can remember when I thought that was a treat. It's a miracle that kids' backs aren't ruined by those mattresses."

One dark eyebrow arched roguishly as Luke smiled down at her. "If you were to sleep here tonight, you could stretch out on a very comfortable king-size bed."

"You *are* feeling better."

"If I'd known you were right down the hall, I might have walked in my sleep."

She knew he was teasing, yet there was a watchful glint in his eyes as if he was waiting to see how she responded. Every time he stood so close...every time he looked at her with that level of intensity... every time he reached out and touched her, tenderly, sensually caressing the curve of her cheek and trailing down the column of her neck . . . her thoughts drifted into dangerous territory. There was a masculinity that never failed to remind her of her own femininity. And there was a strength that drew her to him.

Darcy wasn't the type of woman who sought the protection of a man or wanted to live in his shadow. But with Luke she felt comfortable, so comfortable that she could let her guard down. With Luke she didn't have to try to be anything other than a farm girl from Iowa. There was no pressure and no pretense.

Combined with his other charms, it made him practically irresistible.

Her breath caught in her throat as his expression softened and his eyes focused on her lips. She wanted him to kiss her. She wanted him to ask her to stay with him and spend the night making love in his comfortable king-size bed. She wanted him to ask her to stay in this house with him and his boys forever.

The last thought frightened her more than the first two. She could accept that she had a sexual attraction to Luke. She could even accept a temporary sexual relationship to satisfy that attraction. What she couldn't accept was that she would be tempted to stay *anywhere,* much less podunk Iowa *forever.* She valued her freedom too much. She had worked too hard to get where she was in the broadcasting industry. Nothing could be more foolish than to give it all up for . . . she looked around at the spacious farmhouse's kitchen with its modern appliances and grimaced . . . domesticity. God, she might have to relearn how to cook. And that was definitely close to a blasphemy.

Standing on tiptoe, she pressed a platonic kiss on his cheek. "I can't stay. The boys . . . well, they might ask questions."

He nodded his acceptance, but she saw he wasn't fooled by her excuse. "And there are questions we just don't have the answers to, aren't there?"

She didn't speak because she truly didn't have any answers. And she didn't want to face the questions.

"Good night, Darcy. Thanks for your help."

She hoped her confusion didn't show as she told him good-night and fled into the snow.

But as physically and emotionally exhausted as she was, she lay for hours on her old canopy bed, listening to the rattle of the wind against her window. So many nights she had lain in exactly the same spot thinking of the cute new boy in her algebra class or the high school quarterback who had escorted her to homecoming.

Now, fifteen years later she was lying there, staring at the same white lace trim and the shadows dancing on the wall, thinking about the latest male to make her lose sleep. When she was a teenager, the relationships had seemed so earthshakingly important. But now she knew that had all been a warm-up for the real world. Luke was the real thing. He was steady and dependable. He was successful and self-confident. He was everything she'd ever wanted in a man . . . everything that was good and everything that was frightening.

THE ROW BEHIND the Carsons' was glaringly empty at church on Sunday. Darcy found it even more difficult to concentrate on the service without Luke behind her than when he was. Instead, she spent the entire hour and a half wondering how he and his sons were feeling and if Adam was worse or if Scott had had a relapse or even if there were problems with the turkeys.

*"Darcy, don't be a fool!"* she chastised herself. *"You're letting yourself get too involved with their family. Step back."*

She obeyed her warnings and resisted the urge to stop by Wishbone Acres on her way home from church. Nor did she pick up the telephone and call, even though she found the receiver in her hand several times during the day.

Instead, she tried to immerse herself in her own family, visiting with her sisters-in-law and her nieces and nephews while the men loudly watched a football game in the living room. The snow had continued through the night and, even though it had stopped about noon, the wind was too cold for the children to play outside. When they began getting louder than the men, Darcy took the kids to the barn to play with the two puppies that still hadn't been adopted.

The pony whinnied from her stall, wanting her share of the attention, so Darcy saddled her and let the kids take turns riding around inside the barn.

Bob and Steve and their families left after the game, wanting to get home before dark in case the snow began again as was forecast. Darcy helped her mother in the kitchen, then they both joined her dad to watch the evening news together.

"I really like that anchorwoman. Isn't she cute?" Betty commented.

"Mother, I can't believe you said that!" Darcy exclaimed. "You, of all people, know how women have fought for acceptance because of the way they report the news and not because of the way they look."

"I know, dear," Betty replied, patting her daughter's hand in an appeasing gesture. "But Mindy Farrell is so perky and nice. And ever since she got pregnant, she's gotten even prettier."

"But can she present a story? Can she dig up sources and get good interviews?"

"She never reports on the serious news. They let her do the sweet stories. What do you call them . . . ?"

"Human interest stories," Darcy supplied. "And they're not exactly hard news."

"Don't be so critical, dear. They do things differently in the big cities. Here, we like our news friendly and cheerful."

Darcy rolled her eyes in exasperation. "That's not news, that's 'Entertainment Tonight,' country style. I can't take any more of this. I'm going upstairs to read a book."

But once in her room, she couldn't get interested in any of the reading material left over from her childhood. Trixie Belden and *The Black Stallion* didn't offer the companionship she wanted. She wandered around the room, looking at the football pep rally ribbons and the dried corsages that were pinned next to a montage of photographs on a large bulletin board. Her cheerleader pom-poms hung suspended from the ceiling and a mixed family of stuffed animals sat in chairs, on shelves or on top of the white provincial chest of drawers that matched the four-poster bed.

It was a little girl's room, familiar and comfortable, but somehow upsetting. It reminded her of the bright-eyed idealist she was once, the girl who thought she could have it all, a career, motherhood and the perfect marriage. It reminded her of how many years had passed since she lived in that room and just how old that little girl now was.

Darcy was proud of her achievements. And yet everything she had worked for and struggled to attain was being jeopardized. It was in the hands of a judge who couldn't care less that she had devoted her whole adult life to struggling to reach that point in her career. With the fall of a gavel, it could all be over. The possibility of a fine and even a jail term didn't bother her as much as the thought that she might be faced with losing everything she valued. At thirty-two, she would be starting over.

And if she had to start over, there might be a place in her life for Luke and his boys.

The telephone rang and her mother called up the stairs, "It's for you, Darcy."

"I'll get it in your bedroom," she told her mother as she walked down the hall past the landing. She picked up the receiver and heard her mother hang up. "Hello."

"Hi. Did I interrupt anything?"

At the sound of Luke's voice, the tension in her muscles melted away. "Hi," she answered. "No, I wasn't doing anything important." *Just deciding what to do with the rest of my life,* she added mentally. "We missed your family at church today."

"I didn't want to get the boys out in this weather. So what was the sermon about?"

"It was a continuation of his Count Your Blessings series," she replied, hoping he didn't want her to go into great detail. "I think the gist of it was if the world gives you lemons, you should make lemonade."

"And you were thinking about your lawsuit, weren't you?"

Darcy was taken off guard by his intuitiveness. By admitting that she was worrying about her situation, would that make her seem less in control?

Suddenly it didn't matter. She wanted to talk it over with him. She could use a little of his strength and his wisdom right now.

"Yes, I was thinking about my options."

"Do you think it's going to go against you?"

She shook her head, even though he couldn't see her response through the phone lines. "I wish I knew. I talk to either my agent or my attorney almost every day, but they haven't had anything encouraging to tell me. Sheldon seems to think they're going to use me as an example. They're tired of reporters making news to beef up ratings."

"Who's *they?*"

"The rich and the powerful...the judicial system...everyone who doesn't like reporters who ask too many questions or dig too deep."

"Would a ruling against you bar you from broadcasting?"

"Probably. But even if it didn't, no station would want to hire me. They love controversy...as long as it's happening to someone else so they can report it on the evening newscast."

He was quiet for a moment. "You have other options, you know."

"I've thought of radio and newspapers, but those don't have the excitement of television." She collapsed back against the bed. "I guess I could always write a book about my experiences, but then what?"

"Those things weren't what I had in mind."

"Then what?"

"You could always take a little time off and focus on your personal life." There was another moment of silence on the other end of the phone. "I don't want to sound sexist or anything, but you could let someone else into your life. You might meet a guy and fall in love. Maybe even have a baby or two."

"You make it sound so easy...like I could just pencil it into my datebook. Meet Bob on Monday. Fall in love on Tuesday. Get engaged on Wednesday. Get married on Thursday. Get pregnant on Friday. That would give me Saturday and Sunday to catch up on my mail and the newspapers."

"Bob wasn't the man I had in mind."

A tingle of anticipation trickled through her, making the hair on her arms stand up as if a lightning bolt had just struck nearby. "Who did you have in mind?"

She waited, not breathing, not daring to hope, not even knowing if it was wise of her to pursue this conversation . . . all she knew was that she wanted to hear Luke's answer.

"Oh, I don't know," he said casually. "What about me? As soon as I empty these barns, my calendar's open for the next few months."

With a nonchalance she hoped was equal to his and which was definitely in conflict with the pounding of her heart, Darcy replied, "It sure would make our mothers happy."

"Then that's reason enough to consider it."

"Let's see . . . tomorrow's Monday. What time can we meet?"

# Chapter Eleven

As nervous as a teenager getting dressed for her first prom, Darcy changed clothes a half-dozen times, wishing she'd brought more outfits and all the while knowing she was being silly. Although she hadn't had a serious relationship in years, she dated often. Either he liked her as she was or he didn't.

And since when had it really mattered whether a man liked her?

Since she'd met Luke Calloway.

"Where are you off to today?" Betty asked when Darcy came downstairs after finally deciding on a teal blue cashmere sweater and a pair of black leggings. "It's not even ten o'clock."

"Oh, I thought I might drop in at the Calloway farm and see how everyone's feeling," Darcy answered, carefully avoiding making eye contact with her mother, remembering that Betty had always been able to know when Darcy was telling a fib by looking into her eyes.

"That was Luke on the phone last night, wasn't it?"

"Yes," Darcy answered, choosing not to expand on that answer until she'd had time to have another talk with Luke.

Betty waited expectantly, but Darcy grabbed her purse and coat and tossed her mother a hurried goodbye wave. "I'm not sure when I'll be home. I . . . uh . . . might go on into town and do some shopping."

"I won't wait dinner for you, then."

Darcy dared glance back at her mother and thought she saw a knowing twinkle in the older woman's eyes. Without bothering to put on her coat, she fled the house.

"Pull yourself together, Darcy," she said aloud, giving herself a pep talk on the short drive to Wishbone Acres. But while her brain kept trying desperately to reactivate her logic sensors, her body was trembling with nerves. She felt like she was going to the most important audition of her life.

Luke's truck with the trailer attached was backed up to barn two. Darcy parked her Corvette in the driveway and walked toward the house. She decided to check on Adam first, then maybe Luke would be finished in the barn so they could have their talk.

Joe and Linda met her at the gate and rubbed against her legs, managing to almost trip her with every step. She stopped to rub the puppy's ears, but Linda kept pecking her hand. Darcy had no idea how to deal with a jealous turkey. She had enough trouble trying to figure out her own love life, much less the quirks of frustrated poultry.

The house was quiet, a sharp contrast from the constant noise the three boys had generated while she was staying there. There was always at least one radio, CD player, television or video game on at all times. The house seemed bigger, but much lonelier without the noise of its family.

Darcy looked around the kitchen, noticing breakfast dishes in the sink and pools of spilled milk on the table. She peered into the living room, but the lights were out and the television off. Darcy walked up the stairs, self-consciously tiptoeing so she wouldn't break the eerie silence.

At the top of the stairs she looked toward Nell's room at the right end of the hall, then at Luke's room at the opposite end, and both doors were shut as she'd expected. Greg's room was next to Nell's on the back side of the house and Scott's room was between Greg's and Luke's, also on the back wall. Darcy glanced into Greg's first and saw that it was relatively neat. He had even made the bed although the comforter was crooked, hanging longer on one side than the other.

Darcy looked into Scott's room next and saw the scattered evidence that he had dressed for school. Automatically, she circled the room, closing drawers, tossing toys into the corner toy box, sprinkling a couple of fish food flakes into Sebastian's bowl. But, oddly, Scott's bed was neatly made.

Adam's room was directly across the hall from Scott's and she guessed from the lack of noise that he must be asleep. She didn't want to disturb his rest, so she didn't turn on the light when she crept into the room. The draperies were closed across the window, so she could barely make out his form under a mound of covers on his bed.

If Scott's room had been messy, Adam's looked as if a bomb had exploded in it. As Darcy surveyed the mess, she knew no simple drawer closing and toy tidying would work for that room. Nevertheless, she thought it would help if at least the dirty clothes were picked up off the floor and taken to the hamper.

She made a quick check to confirm that the gerbil and snake were in their cages so she wouldn't find them unexpectedly under the debris. Darcy picked up a sock, two shirts and a pair of jeans and was peering into the semidarkness for the other sock when her foot kicked a heavy metal object.

"Ouch!" she exclaimed, grabbing for what appeared to a trophy of some sort before it toppled over, but the object slid across the tips of her fingers and crashed to the floor. "Darn! Ow! Ow! Ow!" she muttered, still bent down as she squeezed her wounded toes to ease the pain. A glance over at Adam made her feel a little better. Amazingly, the racket hadn't disturbed him.

"Stop right there . . . I have a gun!"

Darcy froze, startled by the unexpected voice. It was low and threatening. Here she was, all alone in the house with a sick kid. Luke was several hundred yards away, inside a barn filled with noisy turkeys. He'd never hear her screams. This intruder could be up to no good. He must have been planning on burglarizing the house. But now his plans had been interrupted. What would he do to her? What would he do to Adam?

Growing more frantic by the second, she tried to think of something to say or do to scare the man off. As she moved her hand, it brushed against the fallen trophy. Automatically, her fingers wrapped around a slender part near its base. Although she had no idea how close the man was, she knew it was her only chance.

She moved quickly, hoping to catch him off guard. Gripping the trophy, she swung it in a wide arc behind her and was gratified to hear the thud of metal against skin, followed by the scrambling of feet and a muffled curse. The man fell forward. Unfortunately, Darcy was directly in his path.

The breath heaved out of her lungs as he landed on her. She couldn't summon even enough air to scream and he had successfully, if accidentally, pinned her arms and legs so she couldn't kick her way free.

The man seemed more intent on his own injuries at first, but all of a sudden, he grew still.

"Darcy?" he asked.

"Luke?" she countered, her voice equally incredulous. "What on earth are you doing here?"

"That's supposed to be my question," he said, pushing himself into a sitting position. "I live here, remember?"

"Well, I know that," she sputtered with growing embarrassment. "But I thought you were in the barn. Your truck is parked over there."

"I got up early today and made a trip to the processor. I wasn't expecting you until eleven."

Darcy's discomfort increased. How could she admit that she'd been so anxious to see him again, to talk to him about the possibility of a future together that it had kept her awake most of the night? When she'd realized she was dressed and ready to go an hour early, she figured she could spend that time with Adam. Taking care of a sick child was guaranteed to take her mind off her own problems. Instead, she decided to put Luke on the defensive.

"You didn't have to threaten me with a gun just because I'm a little early. I thought men liked women who weren't always late."

He stretched toward the nightstand and flipped on the lamp. As the light chased away the shadows, he gave Darcy a crooked grin. "I didn't really have a gun. But don't take my word for it. Feel free to search me."

Darcy's eyes widened as her gaze swept over his body. He was totally nude with the exception of a navy blue bath towel that was wrapped rather precariously around his waist. The sight of all that bare, masculine flesh stretched over a very sexy combination of bulging muscle and sinews left her momentarily speechless.

She sat up as her thoughts tumbled. Still feeling a little silly and awkward at having been caught at what must have appeared to be sneaking around his house, she knew she must say something, so she stated the first thing that popped into her mind. With her attention focused in the general area of his towel, she said, "You know the old question . . . is that a gun under your towel or are you just glad to see me?"

The humor in his eyes simmered into a purely sexual expression. He moved until he was on his hands and knees, straddling her body and forcing her, without touching her, to lie back down on the floor.

"Believe me, I'm *very* glad to see you. And I repeat my suggestion that you can search me. Do with me what you will...." He grimaced as he put his weight on his leg. "Just go easy with my poor bruised leg."

Darcy's body was already trembling from all the tension of the past few minutes. But the rush of adrenaline was replaced by a sensation even more powerful than fear. She looked up at him. He'd obviously just gotten out of the shower. His hair was wet and tousled as if he'd towel dried it, then hastily combed it with his fingers. Tiny droplets of water still clung to his muscular shoulders and chest. She didn't know why she hadn't immediately known he was Luke, but she just hadn't expected him to be there. "I didn't recognize your voice," she murmured. "I thought you were a burglar."

"That was my no-nonsense voice," he replied. "You should hear me when I reprimand the boys. I can sound very fierce."

"I'm sorry about hitting you. And I'm sorry about just walking into your house like that. I honestly thought you were outside working."

"And I thought you were a burglar, too." He kissed the tip of her nose, then gently placed a kiss on each of her eyes, silently encouraging her to close them. "Let me show you what I do to unexpected visitors." He lowered his body over hers until it was touching her from shin to chest although most of his weight was supported with his legs and arms.

She relaxed against the rug, but squirmed when she felt a lump beneath her back. She reached for it and pulled out Adam's jeans. Abruptly, she stiffened.

"Adam! He's right there in the bed, Luke. He'll see us and..."

Luke didn't seem the least bit upset as he traced the curve of her ear with a teasing tongue. "Relax," he murmured. "He's gone to school."

"You mean he isn't in that bed!" she exclaimed. "All the time I was worried that the burglar was going to hurt Adam and me, and Adam wasn't even here!"

He nuzzled against her, nibbling the sensitive skin of her neck. "A tigress protecting her cub. I think that's sweet."

Darcy was so distracted by the feel of his bare skin against her and the caress of his lips that her concern faded. All she could think about was how quickly and completely he could turn her on. She was here to talk about the future, but right now all she cared about was the next few minutes.

His body moved, the extent of his arousal pressing hotly against her. Even with the towel and her layers of clothing between them, she could feel how hard and ready he was. Knowing and feeling his excitement increased her own until nothing mattered but the satisfaction only this man could give her.

Luke's mouth captured hers in a kiss that was at the same instant fierce and tender. "Darcy...Darcy...Darcy..." he murmured between kisses. "This wasn't how I planned to convince you how much you're wanted here. I was going to show you that living in the country can be fun and satisfying. But somehow, every time I get near you, all my good, clean thoughts turn to less wholesome activities. I want you in my life, and I can't deny that I want you in my bed. God, how I want you...."

"I don't know if we can make it work, but I want you, too." Deep within her feminine core, the desire tightened and throbbed, aching for fulfillment. It became more than just a want. It became a need. "Take me," she breathed, her fingers caressing the rippling muscles of his back. "Make love to me...now."

She felt a rush of disappointment as he rolled off her. But he reached down and took her hands in his.

"Let's go to my room. I feel a little intimidated in here with all these posters of Spiderman and Venom watching us, not to mention Adam's creatures."

He pulled her to her feet, holding her against him for a long, deep kiss before leading her into the hall and to his room. Kicking the door shut behind them, he again took her in his arms.

His hands inched under the fuzzy hem of her top and he began lifting it. As soon as the sweater cleared her face, his mouth returned to hers. His hands slid up her arms, pushing the material off until the sweater fell to the floor. But he didn't release her wrists as he held her arms extended above her head.

Slowly, sensually, his fingers stroked down her forearms, over her elbows, along her upper arms to her shoulders. As his hands continued their downward caress, they guided her arms until they looped around his neck.

For a few minutes he was satisfied with the simple pleasure of stroking the bare skin of her back. But finally, he pulled away. He leaned just far enough back so he could let his heated gaze pour over her.

She stood before him, pleased at the passion that flamed in his eyes as he looked at her. Her breasts swelled within the lacy confines of her black bra, begging to be released into his tender loving care.

Luke was trying to show some semblance of control. He thought by breaking physical contact for a few moments, it would ease the inferno that was raging in his groin. It had been years since he'd been to bed with a woman, and he was afraid if he didn't slow down the pace, it would be over much too quickly. With Darcy, he wanted it to last forever.

But as his eyes focused on the soft, lightly tanned skin now exposed, he felt no relief. And he was very aware that the very intimate parts of her anatomy were still hidden by that silly scrap of a bra and those sexy black stretch leggings that looked like they'd been painted on her body.

"If I'd known this might happen, I would have worn something sexy," Darcy said, her wonderful voice curling around him like a whirlpool, pulling him deeper into a vortex from which he couldn't escape . . . as if he would ever want to try.

"Darcy, you'd look sexy in a burlap bag," he managed to respond through his strangely dry throat. "I don't know if I could survive if you looked any sexier than you do right now."

"Let's test that theory." Her eyelids lowered seductively, halfway covering her eyes.

He watched, fascinated as her hands moved to her back, unfastened the bra and let it slide to the floor. His heart forgot how to beat at the sight of her firm, full breasts with their provocative pink nipples pointing toward him, already hard with desire. He wanted to taste those rosy tips and take them into his mouth until they were ready to burst.

Darcy's hands slid under the elastic waistband of her pants, slowly, sensually easing them over her slender hips. It took what seemed like hours for her to peel the black material down her long, beautiful legs. He felt as if all the air had been sucked out of the room as she gracefully lifted one foot at a time and stepped out of the garment.

"Your turn," she breathed huskily.

A flip of his hand tossed his towel to the floor. He held out his arms and Darcy moved into them. As their naked bodies melded together, Luke groaned. Mixed with the passion and his own need for release was the worst case of nerves that he'd experienced in years. It was vitally important to him that he bring pleasure to Darcy. He wanted her to enjoy their lovemaking. More than anything in the world, he wanted her to be happy.

His hand lifted to her chest, not to caress her breast, but to feel her heartbeat. He was reassured when he felt it pounding as wildly and erratically as his own. "Darcy, I..."

She covered his mouth with her fingertips. "Shh...don't say anything. We'll talk later."

They faced the bed, still rumpled from last night. It was obvious that two people had slept there. Darcy glanced at Luke, and he could see the question in her eyes even though she didn't voice it.

"Scott slept with me," he said, offering her the answer without forcing her to ask. "I try to discourage it, but sometimes I don't want to spend the night alone any more than he does."

He flipped the covers back and got into the bed. Propping himself up on his bent elbow, he held out his other hand. "No other woman has ever been in this bed," he said softly, again answering her unspoken questions. "Let's initiate it together."

She placed her hand in his and slid across the bed until she was lying next to him. Luke rummaged around in his nightstand drawer and pulled out protection that was so old he hoped it would still be effective. Darcy surprised him by taking it and gently pulling it on his stiffened member.

Her touch was almost more than he could bear. He shifted so he was on top, his legs straddling hers. There was so much he wanted to say, but he remembered her request that he not voice his feelings yet. He didn't know if that was because she didn't share those feelings and was doing this just for the pleasure, or if she didn't want to make any sort of commitment. And right now, he didn't want to think about her reasons. He didn't want to think at all. He just wanted to feel.

He tunneled his fingers through her sparkling hair and spread it out on the white pillowcase. She was smiling up at him encouragingly, affectionately, and he dared hope this meant as much to her as it did to him. Lowering his head, he moved his lips over hers, trying to express his feelings in the kiss.

The thrust of her breasts against his chest reminded him there were many parts of her body that he hadn't sampled. His hand blazed the way, stroking, exploring. His lips followed, trailing down her neck, then up the peak of her breast until he captured, at last, the sweetness of that pink treasure. Pulling her nipple into his mouth, he cupped it with his tongue, suckling it until she cried aloud. Her fingers dug into his hair, holding his head down while her body arched upward.

He turned his attention to her other breast as his fingers caressed the taut skin of her stomach and then became tangled in the soft curls below before finally slipping into her warmth.

But feeling how wet and ready she was for him was the straw that snapped his control. He nudged his knees between her legs, centering himself over her as he moved up. Bracing himself on his arms, he looked down at her lovely face, savoring for a moment the beauty and strength of her features. The feelings he had for her were more than mere desire. He knew, to his delight . . . and his dismay . . . that he loved her.

As he eased himself inside her, his heart swelled with the emotion he had for this woman. It made their lovemaking all the more wonderful. Slowly, he pushed deeper, knowing it wouldn't take too many thrusts before he wouldn't be able to hold back. He didn't know if he'd ever be able to experience this moment ever again, so he didn't want to hurry. But Darcy's hands gripped his buttocks, urging him to move faster.

It took only two more strokes for her to reach her climax. She cried his name and bucked beneath him. From deep inside he could feel the ripples of her orgasm and he knew he no longer had to hold back. With a groan of release he rocketed to the moon. Hugging her tightly he knew he would never willingly let her go.

"Luke..." Darcy spoke softly, her breath stirring his tousled hair. For several minutes they had been lying quietly, catching their breath and trying to let their emotions catch up with their bodies.

"Hmm," he answered, so completely drained from the intensity of their union that he could barely speak.

"I...I'm not as...experienced as you might think." Her words came out haltingly and almost shyly.

"I never thought you were," he denied, although, in truth, the thought had never been far from his mind. She was beautiful, young, eligible and smack in the middle of a fast-paced life-style. Of course, he'd assumed she was not celibate. But he'd refused to let himself think about just how many men might have experienced with her what he just had.

"I guess all those talks my mother used to give me and all those Sunday School lessons I used to hear must have soaked in." She moved back until she could look directly into his eyes. "I just wanted you to know that this was very special for me. I date a lot, but I don't sleep around."

He tried not to let the relief and pleasure that news gave him show. Instead, he replied with outward calm, "You didn't have to tell me that...but I'll admit I'm glad. This meant a lot to me. Darcy, I..." He hesitated, not wanting to rush her, but unable to hold back all of his feelings to her. "I could easily fall in love with you," he said, settling for a declaration as close to the truth as possible. What he wouldn't tell her was that it was already a fait accompli.

"Yes, I feel that way, too. But Luke, I can't make any promises. Not yet."

"I'm not asking you to." *It would only kill me if you leave.*

"But I do want to spend as much time as possible with you and the boys." She pushed her hair back from her face and stared up at the ceiling. "I'm so confused. I know I want my job, but..." her voice trailed off as she shook her head and gave him a bewildered smile "...but I never counted on meeting you."

SHE WALKED ALONG a pathway that had been cleared through the snow. From the sounds coming from the barn, it was obvious the turkeys were being disturbed.

Darcy cautiously opened the door and peeked inside. Luke noticed her immediately and waved.

"Grab a stick and help me," he called loudly so he could be heard above the gobbles and yelps.

She glanced down at her lace-trimmed pants and the ballerina slippers she'd put back on after taking a quick shower. No other man she'd ever known would have asked such a thing. But then no other man she'd ever known was Luke.

She noticed a pair of rubber boots outside the door. They were so large she was able to slip her feet inside without taking off her shoes. It was a challenge lifting her feet without losing the boots, but she managed to clomp along, waving her stick the way Luke was. The turkeys were surprisingly easy to herd, due, no doubt, to their limited intelligence. They moved in a large group through the side door and into the trailer. Luke positioned Darcy by the door while he rounded up three turkeys who were either smarter or much stupider than the rest. After only fifteen minutes, the barn was empty.

"I've got to take these guys to the processor," Luke said. "I wanted to make one more trip before the boys get home. You could ride with me...if you don't mind another trip in the old truck."

"I think I can handle that." She kicked off the boots and was about to tiptoe through the snow to the truck's passenger side door when Luke stepped forward and swept her into his arms, lifting her off the ground and carrying her across the space.

He opened the door and set her on the blanket-covered seat, not letting go of her as he leaned into the cab and gave her a long, slow kiss.

"Is that how you thank all the women who help you with your turkeys?" she asked a little breathlessly.

"There aren't many women who are interested in helping out around a turkey farm."

"It's their loss. You should advertise. They'd be out here in swarms."

He leveled a steady look at her. "I'm not interested in attracting swarms of women."

"Oh?"

"No," he answered. "All I want is one."

"Oh." Darcy couldn't hold back a relieved grin.

"If you keep looking at me like that, we'll never get these turkeys to the processor," he promised, his voice low and husky. He slid one hand along her thigh.

Darcy was truly tempted. But they'd already made love several times and they'd both been afraid they would fall asleep and still be lying naked in his bed when the boys got home from school. It was not something they thought any of his children were quite ready to understand. But she couldn't resist kissing him again before she turned to face forward so he could shut the door.

After double-checking the latch on the trailer, Luke climbed into the driver's side and started the engine.

"I'll bet Adam wasn't thrilled to get to go to school today. I think he was hoping to milk a couple more days out of his illness."

"Unfortunately for him, he didn't have as bad a case as Scott or I did." Luke gave her a very intimate glance. "But I'm sure glad he went to school. Although I have no idea how I'm going to explain how his Little League trophy got broken."

Darcy chuckled and leaned back against the blanket-covered seat, but immediately bolted upright as an uncoiled spring stuck her in the shoulder.

Luke noticed her discomfort and suggested, "You could scoot a little more to the center of the seat. I don't think it's as uncomfortable there."

"I've heard my share of lines, but that one is definitely the most original."

Luke grinned down at her as she scooted closer. "Why do you think I keep this old bucket of bolts?" He draped his arm around her shoulders. "You'll have to shift for me."

"Lord, I haven't done this since high school," she said, moving the stick shift to third gear as he stepped on the clutch.

"Yeah, well, that's how I feel right now." He squeezed her arm. "Like I'm about eighteen years old."

She nodded. "Yes, so do I, and it's a great feeling. Lately I've felt very old and unimportant in the overall scheme of life."

"Lucky for you I like old things."

Darcy swatted his leg with the back of her hand. "You were supposed to say that I'm not old or unimportant."

He stared directly into her eyes and said, "If you're fishing for meaningless compliments, you've come to the wrong place. But if you're looking for a man who will love and take care of you and a life that is as close to normal as it can be with three boys, an obnoxious puppy and a neurotic pet turkey, then you're sitting in the right truck."

Darcy blinked. She had no idea how to respond to such a direct statement. She was used to playing flirtatious word games. But, she would be wise to remember that this man was playing for keeps.

They arrived at the huge processing plant and Darcy waited in the coffee room while the turkeys were unloaded and added to Luke's account.

On the way back to the farm, they stopped at the local Chinese restaurant and picked up a half-dozen cartons to take home for dinner. Since she'd skipped breakfast and she and Luke had been busy all day with lunch being the last thing on their minds, Darcy realized she was very hungry. When they arrived at his house, he parked the rusty old truck next to her shiny red Corvette. Neither Luke nor Darcy remarked on the striking contrast although it was impossible not to notice.

"I've got to take a quick shower," Luke said as he glanced at his watch. "Scott and Adam should already be home and Greg will be here any minute. I'll hurry so we can all have a total family experience."

Darcy slid him an amused look. "I've spent more time with kids in the past week than I have in the last few years," she added.

"We're a package deal, you know," he said, suddenly serious. "I couldn't fall in love with a woman who didn't want my children. They're very much a part of me."

"Yes, I know." Darcy knew it would be a huge adjustment to her life-style should she and Luke actually move in together. But she was willing to give it a chance.

Luke opened the back gate and they maneuvered around the obstacle course of wiggling puppy and jealous turkey.

"I guess I can assume that Joe is going to stay?" Darcy asked.

"Scott used his big blue eyes and his most persuasive *please Daddy* on me. I guess a kid deserves something special every once in a while." Luke held the back door open and sneaked a quick kiss as she stepped past him. "And I've just realized, so does his dad."

## Chapter Twelve

"What if it's just a sexual attraction?" Darcy stretched, very conscious of the arousing friction of her bare skin against his. Although she'd slipped away to meet him in their private paradise for the last three days, she was afraid their passion wouldn't be enough. "We can't spend the rest of our lives in bed."

They lay side by side on his bed with her back pressed against his chest. His arms were wrapped around her, holding her close with his chin resting on her shoulder.

"As much as I'd like to do just that, I'm afraid I'd be forced to get up every once in a while to take care of the turkeys and to get the boys off to school."

"I hate reality checks," Darcy complained.

"Speaking of which, have you heard from your agent or your attorney lately?"

"Not since last week. And in this case, no news isn't necessarily good news."

Luke didn't comment as he rubbed his cheek against her neck and idly stroked the smooth curve of her hip.

"A penny for your thoughts," Darcy said, hating his silence. It was not the comfortable, companionable silence they often shared, but a strained, heavy hush.

Instead of addressing the issue, he pressed a kiss into the shadowy hollow of her neck and rolled to the edge of the bed. "I'd better get to work. This is my busy season, and here we are, lying around in bed."

Darcy pulled the sheet up under her arms and sat up, watching as Luke dressed. "I'm sorry I *wasted* all your precious time. I won't come over here again since you're so busy."

He jerked the zipper up on his jeans with a little more force than was necessary, then sucked in a deep, steadying breath.

"Dammit, Darcy. What do you want me to say?" he demanded. "Do you want me to get on my knees and beg you to stay and risk having you hate me for asking? Do you want me to kiss you goodbye, wish you well with your life in L.A. and forget you? Do you want me to wait for your infrequent visits so we can fall into bed, then I can take you to the airport so you can jet off to God knows where?" He lifted his hands, palms up in a frustrated gesture. "I just don't know what you want."

Darcy drew her knees up and rested her chin on her crossed arms. "Neither do I," she admitted. "All I know is that I really care about you and your family. I didn't think I'd ever consider coming back to Greenhaven to live. And I sure didn't think I'd ever meet a man like you here."

"So where does that leave us? I don't want you to go to prison, but I don't want you to get your job back, either. And it doesn't really matter what I want anyway, does it?'' He picked up his shirt, but instead of putting it on, he wadded it into a ball and clenched it in his fists as he stared down at her. "This is not just sex for me. I think you and I could make it, but I'm not going to sit around forever, waiting for you to make up your mind."

Darcy stood up, pulling the sheet around her as she approached Luke. One hand gripped the edges of the sheet together above her breasts while her other hand reached out to stroke the hard set of his jaw. "I'm trying to work through so many things right now. Please be patient...this is *your* house, *your* family, *your* world. *I'm* the one who's having to make all the changes...and, believe me, these are pretty drastic changes for me."

His jaw softened beneath her touch and the steely edge left his eyes. "Darcy, you make me crazy."

Darcy's fingers threaded through the hair curling at the nape of his neck. "I just want to make you happy. For now, that's enough."

He looped his arms around her waist and pulled her against him. "You'll be here until at least Thanksgiving, right?"

She nodded.

"Then we'll take advantage of the time we have left. I won't beg you to stay. But maybe by then, you won't want to go."

She released the sheet and it slithered to the floor. "Maybe by then, I'll be begging you to let me stay."

DARCY WAS MAKING the bed when the phone began ringing. Luke was outside, loading the last of the turkeys in barn one.

She glanced at the phone, hesitating a moment as she wondered whether or not she should answer it. After all, it wasn't her place to be answering Luke's phone. On the other hand, it could be her mother or even Nell. Or it might even be Sheldon or Charlie calling about the case after getting Luke's number from her mother.

Her hand hovered over the receiver, then she snapped it up. "Hello."

"Darcy?" asked a small voice.

"Yes. Is this Scott?"

"Yeah, it's me. I'm at school."

"Uh . . . did you want to talk to your dad?"

"I need some jigglers."

"Some what?"

"Jigglers . . . you know those things we eat with our fingers."

Darcy didn't have a clue what jigglers were, but before she could ask, Scott continued, his voice a little frantic.

"It's my turn to bring snacks and I forgot. I really *have* to have some jigglers by recess. Could you bring me some? Please, Darcy? Everyone will be really mad at me if we don't have snacks."

"Sure, Scott, I'll bring you some jigglers. What time is recess?"

He turned away from the phone and she could hear him asking the office worker. When he returned to Darcy he said, "One-fifteen."

"I'll be there. Don't worry."

There was an audible sigh of relief. "I've got to go to music now. Bye."

Darcy hung up the phone, but immediately called her mother. When there was no answer, she debated what her next course of action should be. She was a resourceful woman. Surely, she could discover what a jiggler was and come up with enough to feed Scott's class.

A search of the refrigerator and the pantry didn't reveal anything. She knew she could go to the barn and ask Luke, but this was almost like a test of her motherhood abilities so she hated to admit that she didn't know something that was probably a staple of children's diets.

Susan. She would know. Darcy picked up the phone and dialed her secretary's number. And, of course, Susan did know what jigglers were. A few minutes later Darcy was stirring several boxes of gelatin together with boiling water and feeling very pleased with her initiative. She wasn't too bad at this mothering business after all.

"LET'S TRY TO THINK of something we can all do together," Luke suggested.

"Monopoly."

"Dr. Mario."

"Dungeons and Dragons."

It was Friday evening and Darcy was sitting in the Calloway living room with Luke and his sons as they debated what to do for family night. The boys were assembled with various levels of enthusiasm for the weekly event with Scott jumping around with his usual irrepressible energy, Greg lounging on the couch with his usual expression of boredom and Adam sitting on the edge of a chair trying not to appear interested, but almost as eager as Scott.

"Let's do something different," Luke insisted.

"Miniature golf," Adam suggested.

"Burger King," Greg offered.

"Let's go bowling." Scott bounced up and down. "I want to show Darcy how good I can bowl."

"Yes, bowling," Adam added his second to the unofficial motion.

Luke turned to Darcy. "You probably haven't even seen a bowling alley for years."

"Are you kidding?" she replied with a grin. "Every small town in this hemisphere has a bowling alley. It's a great way to pass the time when I'm stuck out in the middle of nowhere waiting for a story to develop."

"Then bowling it is. Everyone, get your coats and get into the car."

"Dad, you're not serious!" Greg exclaimed with genuine horror. "We're not *all* going to a public place, are we?"

"It's not a crime to go out with your family," Luke informed him sternly.

"Well, I don't want to go," Greg stated flatly.

"This is family night, and you're going with us." Luke was equally adamant.

Darcy knew some of Greg's lack of cooperation was due to his age. But she also knew that some of it was due to her presence.

"Look, this is a family thing," she said. "I don't have to go."

Luke spun around. "Yes, you do," he answered aloud. But she could read a deeper message in his eyes. If she was ever to be a part of this family, now was the time to join in. He was challenging her decision to make the effort.

Darcy nodded. It was as important to her that she be accepted as it was to him. She walked toward Scott and Adam. "We'll wait in the car," she told Luke.

Adam and Scott sat in the back seat, unusually quiet as they kept a close watch on the garage door. When it finally opened and both Greg and Luke walked toward the car, it was as if everyone began breathing again.

The bowling alley was almost full and Luke got the last two lanes that were available. The boys put on their rented shoes and began searching for a bowling bowl. Darcy hung back with Luke.

"Maybe it would be better if I didn't bowl," she offered. "I could keep score or something. I really don't mind."

"I can't force you to bowl with us, but I really wish you would. You can't take Greg's temper tantrum personally."

"He's having trouble accepting me."

"He's having trouble with everything right now except his friends and his role-playing games. I realize he's going through an uncomfortable phase, but I'm not going to let him rule the household."

Darcy didn't want to be caught in the middle of a father-son conflict. But she knew it went much deeper than just having her around. Long before she had arrived on the scene, there had been a power struggle going on as Greg stretched his wings and tried to fly.

"Then prepare to be beaten," Darcy remarked. "On the bowling lanes, that is."

She and Luke found balls from the racks and carried them to their lanes. Adam and Scott were already warming up while Greg sat sullenly, pretending not to watch. The air was so thick with tension, she almost bumped into it as she sat down across from Greg and replaced her boots with the rented shoes.

Suddenly, they were surrounded by a dozen teenagers, all of whom knew Greg but were obviously trying to get a good look at the biggest local celebrity in Greenhaven's history. Darcy watched Greg's reaction as the kids prodded him to introduce them. Finally, he complied, but did nothing to hide his reluctance.

Darcy signed a few autographs and recounted a couple of stories about meeting teenage celebrities. And she could see that while the kids were impressed, Greg was growing more distant by the moment.

"It was nice meeting all of you," Darcy said, stepping up to the ball return. "But I think I'm holding up the game."

"Wow, Greg," Darcy heard one of them whisper. "She's really cool. And what a babe. You're so lucky that she's dating your dad. She might even introduce you to Charlie Sheen."

When Darcy returned to her seat after delighting Scott with a strike, she noticed Greg was observing her with an odd, measuring look. But before she could read anything in his expression, he got up and took his turn.

They continued through the lineup, changing lanes and getting confused with the scoring. Even Greg began to lose his attitude and enjoy himself.

Darcy cradled the battered black ball in her hands, took several measured steps forward and propelled it toward the pins.

"It's another strike!" Scott shouted.

"I can't believe it. She's beating us," Adam complained with good-natured humor. "Dad, you're not going to let a woman beat us guys, are you?"

"I don't see what I can do about it." Luke gave Darcy a fierce scowl. "I didn't know she was a ringer."

"I tried to warn you," Darcy said with a laugh. "I don't like to spend my spare time in bars. Besides, I pick up a lot of information at bowling alleys."

"You must not be a very important reporter," Greg commented, lifting his belligerent gaze to meet Darcy's, "or you'd be going to exciting places."

"Like Paris, London, Melbourne, Beirut and Riyadh?" Darcy asked. "I've been there. But I've also been to Alvin, Texas to interview Nolan Ryan and to the Carolinas when they had a hurricane and Grand Junction, Colorado when a lot of their refineries shut down. Being a good reporter doesn't mean I get all the glamour jobs. I'll go anywhere there's a good story."

"So I guess that means you won't be hanging around in Greenhaven very long." Greg picked up his ball and approached the lanes. "Nothing exciting *ever* happens here."

"You're leaving?" Scott asked, his blue eyes huge with dismay. "But I thought you were going to live with us."

"Yeah, you like it here, don't you?" Adam asked, unable to hide his own disappointment.

Darcy and Luke exchanged startled glances.

"Darcy's waiting until after Thanksgiving to decide. You're next, Scotty," Luke said, changing the subject.

Darcy kept score until it was her turn again.

"Get a turkey, Darcy," Adam called.

"A turkey? What does that mean?" she asked, glancing over her shoulder at him.

"It's three strikes in a row," Adam explained.

"We're turkey experts," Scott stated proudly.

Darcy's ball again found its mark, sending all ten pins scattering into the pit.

"You did it!" Adam exclaimed. "Now you can't leave. Anybody who can bowl turkeys should live at Wishbone Acres."

Darcy laughed and scooted onto the chair next to Luke behind the score table.

"Three down, one to go," Luke whispered for her ears only, then he picked up the pencil and colored in the appropriate square on the score sheet.

Darcy didn't pretend not to know that he was referring to the conquering of the Calloway clan and not the game. And as pleased as she was at the victory, she wondered if it would ever be possible for her to win Greg over.

"So HOW ARE things going at the farm? I'm sure Luke isn't telling me everything. And there's a suspiciously cheerful note in his voice lately."

"Nell, I wish I knew," Betty responded. "All I can tell you is that Darcy has been leaving awfully early every morning and not coming home until late at night. But she hasn't said anything about what's going on in the hours in between."

"What's wrong with kids nowadays!" Nell exclaimed with a great deal of aggravation. "When they're teenagers you worry constantly about them experimenting with the birds and the bees. And now that they're older, they've lost interest."

"Maybe it's too soon to give up hope. I know Darcy's been spending a lot less time talking about her job and the court case. And I even found some turkey feathers on her coat the other night."

"Turkey feathers . . . that's a good sign. If Luke's taken her to the barn, then it must be getting serious."

"I hate to say this, but I'm more interested in him taking her to bed."

"Betty! I'm shocked," Nell declared, but she neutralized any hint of disapproval with a chuckle.

"I've always believed that all Darcy needed to bring her home was a good man."

"That's my Luke. I just wish he wasn't such a slow worker. We have only two weeks left before Thanksgiving."

Betty sighed. "I know. And I'm getting worried that I'm going to lose my daughter again."

"Don't give up. At their age, it just takes a little longer for the birds and the bees to get buzzing."

"BY THE END OF THE WEEK I'll be finished with all of my Thanksgiving turkeys. Four barns will be completely empty." Luke leaned back, braced against the railing post on his porch.

"Will you sell all the turkeys in the two other barns for Christmas?" Darcy held out some crumbled bread and Linda strutted up to pick it daintily off her palm. "Or do you keep some of the stock for breeding?"

"I sell off completely in December," Luke explained, trying to ignore the puppy, but unable to resist playing tug-of-war with Joe's favorite rubber squeaky toy. "And I don't restock until March."

"March! You take two *months* off! What a cushy job," Darcy teased.

"And I usually take July off, too, so I can go someplace special with the boys while they're out for summer vacation," he bantered in return. "I'll bet you don't get that kind of vacation where you work."

"Are you kidding? I haven't had a real lie-on-the-beach-and-drink-margaritas vacation in five years."

"Neither have I, but that's just because the boys like more active vacations like Disneyland or hiking through Yellowstone."

Darcy took another slice of stale bread out of a bag and tore it into little pieces for Linda. "But I don't really miss the time off because I don't have a nine-to-five job even when I'm at the station every day. That sort of schedule would drive me crazy."

"Me, too. That's another of the reasons I enjoy the farm. Even though I have to stick pretty close seven days a week while the barns are full, I can set my own hours. And about seventy-five percent of my income is in the fall, so the rest of the year when I have a flock, I don't have to operate but at about half capacity." He tossed the toy out in the yard and Joe scrambled after it, retrieving it with instincts that had been bred into him for generations. "Then on the months off I have time to clean and disinfect the barns and get ready for the next flock."

"So you buy the baby turkeys and raise them?"

"Yes, they're about six to eight weeks old when I bring them here. I've thought about experimenting with breeding, but domestic turkeys can't mate because of their weight and broad breasts, so it all has to be done artificially. Right now there are only about four companies in the world who provide eggs for the hatcheries. The eggs have to be watched closely and rotated for twenty-eight days. Then it takes another two or three days for the poults to break out of their shell. That might be a little more trouble than I'm willing to handle. Plus there's the vaccinations, desnoodings and all the other things that have to be done to them when they're only a few days old."

Darcy looked around at the expensive buildings, the vast open land and the almost new car in the driveway. She knew from her parents' income that farm profits were unpredictable, but could provide a comfortable income if managed properly and if there wasn't a run of bad luck.

"You've got a real nice setup here," she commented.

They relaxed and enjoyed the unseasonably warm November sun that was doing an excellent job of melting away the last patches of snow from the storm. Joe tirelessly fetched every object Luke would throw while Linda kept begging for more food. When they tired of humoring the humans, they began playing together.

Darcy watched with amusement as Joe carried the turkey around in his mouth. Even more bizarre, Linda seemed to enjoy the game as she lay limply until Joe set her down. Immediately, she would hop to her feet, shake herself and start pecking specks of dried grass and dirt off his fur.

"I've never seen anything like that," she remarked.

"Neither have I."

"Why is Linda brown when all the rest of your turkeys are white?"

"She was a throwback. I raise a breed called the Broad-Breasted Large White. They're a cross between the Broad-Breasted Bronze and White Holland. White turkeys aren't albinos, but have a recessive gene that prevents pigmentation everywhere except their eyes so they don't have the weaknesses that albinos usually have. And white turkeys bring more money at market because colored pigment sometimes soaks into the skin leaving dark spots."

"So Linda wouldn't have brought as much money as a white female her age and size?"

"No, because her meat wouldn't have looked as clean and appealing as the others, even though, technically, there's nothing wrong with her. That's why I held her back for our own dinner. Besides, we don't need a really large turkey for our family."

Darcy gasped. Surely, she'd misunderstood him. "You're not still planning on eating . . . I mean, Linda isn't still going to be the main course at Thanksgiving, is she?"

"I wish you wouldn't call her that. She's not a pet—she's food."

Darcy pushed herself to her feet and stared down at Luke with horror. "But Linda's different. The boys will be devastated . . . especially Scott. You're not *really* going to kill her, are you?"

Luke stood up and gripped her forearms. "Come on, Darcy. You're a farm girl. You know the difference between a pet and livestock. I can't let a full-grown turkey run loose in my yard."

"Why not?"

"Well, I don't know. I just can't," he declared. "It's just not good business."

Darcy looked out at the dog and the turkey as they continued to play their own version of tag. In her head she understood his reasoning, but in her heart she couldn't bear the thought of Linda on a platter.

"Don't get all sentimental about this," Luke continued. "Greg and I are going pheasant hunting this weekend. Adam and Scott were supposed to stay home with Mom, but now, I guess they'll be going, too. Why don't you come with us? It'll help you remember that birds are supposed to be food."

"I don't know."

"You're not against hunting, are you?"

"I understand and accept it in principle. My dad used to take my brothers deer hunting every winter. I was a real tomboy back then and I could outshoot both Sam and Bob on the gun range. So I insisted on going along."

Darcy shook her head. "I loved the camping and sitting out in the woods watching the animals. But when it came to actually lining up a deer in my rifle sight and pulling the trigger, I realized it was a whole different thing to shoot at a living creature instead of a paper target."

"So you liked the hunting, but not the killing."

"That's pretty much it. And it's not because I think there's anything wrong about it as long as it's for food and not just for sport."

"That's my point. I raise turkeys for food, not sport, and certainly not for pets."

Darcy was still not mollified.

"Let's not argue about this," Luke said. "But I would like you to seriously think about coming hunting with us. You can stay in camp if you want, but I think you'll enjoy walking with us. And it'll be good for Greg to have a chance to get to know you a little better."

Darcy hesitated, tempted to go along simply because she wanted to be with Luke and it was a good idea to spend more time with Greg. "It's been a long time since I did any camping," she mused.

Luke inched closer and twisted a thick tendril of her hair around his finger. "We'll have to have separate sleeping bags. But I'll make it up to you on a private camp-out of our own later."

"Hmm, I've never made love in a sleeping bag."

"I'll keep that in mind," he promised as he dropped a kiss on the tip of her nose.

# Chapter Thirteen

"I'm not going," Greg stated emphatically. "It's embarrassing enough for you and her to be *dating*. There's no way I'm going to spend the whole weekend with her."

Even after forcing himself to silently count to ten, Luke had difficulty controlling his anger. "We've been planning this weekend for six months, and you're going to go."

"That's just it... *we've* been planning it. And now *she's* horning in." Greg didn't back down as he stood almost as tall as his father. "I don't like her, and I don't want to be around her."

Luke's anger faded, only to be replaced by bewilderment. How could anyone be around Darcy and not fall in love with her? He'd certainly fought against it, but she had easily won him over. Why was Greg immune? "Darcy is a terrific lady. She's done everything she can to get along with you boys. Adam and Scott don't have any problems with her."

"I guess they're not as picky as I am about who they spend their time with." Greg added with a disgusted snort, "And I never would have thought you'd fool around with someone like that."

"Like what?" Luke asked, pressing to get to the truth beneath Greg's attitude.

"You know . . . someone so fancy."

It began to dawn on Luke just where the problem might lie. "You mean someone so unlike your mother."

"Well, yeah, that's part of it," Greg admitted. "I don't see how you could be interested in someone so different from Mom."

"You might be surprised to hear this, but your mother and Darcy have many of the same qualities. They're both very pretty, sweet, generous women. It's probably difficult for you to understand the different levels of my relationships with them. I met your mother when she was young and innocent and we grew up together as we started our family. But Darcy and I are older and have other things in common."

"So your own kids aren't as important to you as your girlfriend." Beneath the censure in Greg's statement was a quiver of insecurity.

Luke wanted to reach out and hug Greg, but the distance between him and his son was more than mere air. Luke wondered when the wall had been built. When Greg was younger, he had sat in Luke's lap and listened to stories and talked about everything from bad dreams to best friends. But at some point, the communication had halted. Now, even when they talked, they weren't communicating.

Darcy and Scott entered the room, chatting about Joe's latest trick, and Greg immediately withdrew even further.

"We'll talk about this later," Luke said, lowering his voice so only Greg could hear. "But you *are* going hunting with us."

Greg challenged his father with a glare, but he didn't speak as he whirled around and stalked out of the room.

"What was that all about?" Darcy asked.

Luke hesitated, considering whether or not he should tell Darcy how Greg felt. "Greg doesn't want to go camping." Luke chose a half-truth, but avoided meeting her gaze as he answered.

Darcy studied him, then commented with a perception that had been, no doubt, honed by her job, "He's not crazy about having an outsider along, is he?"

"You're not an outsider," Luke protested.

"Of course I am. And I always will be to Greg because he's too old to accept change within his family without a lot of adjustment. His memories of his mother are sharper than Adam's and Scott's, so naturally any other woman will never measure up."

Luke wished he could be as understanding. "If things turn out the way I'm hoping they will, Greg will have to accept you as a part of the family."

Darcy's beautiful lips curved into a smile. "If you don't mind, I think I'll help things move along. I'm going to talk to him."

"I don't know if that would be..."

Darcy silenced him with a determined look. "It won't hurt for me to try."

Luke shrugged, but he didn't have much hope for her success. "Scott and I are going to be doing chores and putting his turkey up for the night." He stood in the entry hall and watched her walk up the stairs. The sexy sway of her hips encased in a pair of the tightest jeans in Iowa made him pause and watch with voyeuristic pleasure. At the top step, she glanced over her shoulder and gave him a knowing wink, confirming his suspicion that there was very little that would escape her notice. But still, he doubted she'd be able to break through to Greg.

Darcy knocked on Greg's door and waited for his response.

"Who's there?"

"It's me, Darcy. May I come in and talk to you for a few minutes?"

There was a long moment's silence before the door opened. He made no effort to sound welcoming as he said, "I'm busy. I've got lots of homework and—"

"This won't take long." She shut the door behind her and sat on his desk chair after he flopped down on the bed. "I know you're not too crazy about me, and I want you to know that's okay. I'm not your mother...I'm not anyone's mother, so I'm not too sure how to relate to children. But you're almost grown, so I think you and I can be absolutely honest with each other."

Greg was doodling on one of his book covers and didn't appear to be paying attention, but Darcy continued with the hope that some of what she said might soak in.

"Your father is a grown man, and he has the right to have a life of his own. Just because he and I might someday marry doesn't mean you, Adam and Scott won't always be the most special people in his life. I would never try to push you guys aside. If you can't accept me as a friend, then at least try to tolerate me as a friend of the family."

"You say that now, but once you move in, you'll take over," Greg countered, still not looking up from his sketches.

Darcy glanced around the room and noticed several very intricate pencil drawings mounted on the walls next to a set of the *Star Wars* trilogy posters. "I would never make any big changes. I know I'm the new kid on the block, and I'm going to try to fit in rather than make waves."

"But you're already butting in on our camping trip."

"Your father asked me to go, and I didn't think you or the other boys would mind. I thought that if I was there I could watch Adam and Scott so you and your dad could spend all day hunting."

Greg heaved a depressed sigh and rolled over on his back with his arm thrown across his eyes to block out the light and her searching gaze.

Darcy watched him carefully, interpreting his body language. It was a skill she'd developed to get her through those difficult interviews. Finally, it dawned on her what part of the problem was.

"You don't want to go hunting, do you?"

He lifted his arm just enough so he could peer at her with one eye. "Sure, I do. My dad's been counting on this for months."

"I didn't ask if your dad wanted to go. I asked if *you* did." He didn't answer, so she continued, "I used to go hunting with my father, but I never shot anything. My brothers made fun of me, calling me a sissy because I let quite a few nice bucks pass within range."

"This is my first hunt," Greg muttered. "Dad wants me to go with him again when deer season opens in December."

"You don't have to kill anything. In fact, you don't even have to shoot your gun. I know from experience that it's the fun of being out there together, as a family. It's amazing what we could talk about over a campfire . . . things we never would have discussed at home. No matter how busy we were or how far apart we'd drifted, those hunting trips always brought us home closer together."

"Nah, my dad and I don't have anything in common. He doesn't understand my interest in . . . things," he finished evasively.

"You like to draw, don't you?" Darcy walked across the room and viewed one of the sketches. "This is yours, isn't it?"

"Yeah, it's just something I scribbled while I was on the phone."

"It's very good. You've got a good eye for detail and balance. Have you taken any art classes?"

"A few." The arm slid away from his eyes and he sat up. "But I really like to write stories, especially science fiction."

"I've taken a lot of courses in writing. Maybe I could look at some of your work sometime."

His eyes narrowed as if he was measuring her sincerity.

"And you think your dad wouldn't approve of your artistic skill?" Darcy guessed.

"He wouldn't think it was anything I could do as a career. He wants me to get a degree in engineering or agriculture so I'll have something to fall back on."

"That's not a bad idea, but surely there's a subject that interests your creative side. How about computers? Believe it or not, operating a computer uses the creative part of the brain just like drawing or writing."

"Really?"

Darcy nodded. "Look, I'll make a deal with you." The skeptical curtain fell back across his eyes.

"If you'll go on this camp-out with your dad, try to keep an open mind and see if you two guys can have a real conversation, I'll stay at home with Scott and Adam."

"What makes you think Dad will agree to that?"

"I'll talk to him about it. He's really very understanding. I think you'll be surprised at how much the two of you are alike." Darcy leaned against Greg's dresser as she explained, "His father pushed him to get a degree in dentistry when all Luke wanted was to live on a farm. Give him a chance."

Greg frowned as if she had presented him with a totally new concept. "Maybe it wouldn't be too bad. After all, it's only for the weekend."

"Good. I'll tell your father about your decision. And remember . . . have fun."

AFTER A QUIET EVENING of eating pizza, coaching Scott on his lines for his class's Thanksgiving re-enactment and playing games, Darcy figured she had this motherhood thing under control. Adam and Scott got along together amazingly well with only a couple of arguments to mar a perfect night.

As Darcy lay in Nell's queen-size bed, wishing she was in Luke's bed with him at her side, she wondered how he and Greg were getting along. She hoped her advice to Greg hadn't been overly optimistic. On the other hand, she had every confidence that Luke would listen to Greg. Actually, she had more faith in the campfire. No one could sit around a crackling fire with the star-studded sky above and not tell the truth. It was nature's best lie detector. It reduced the most complex problems to their simplest forms. Perhaps Luke and Greg would be able to find some neutral ground and help each other get through the next few difficult years.

Luke hadn't been too pleased about the change in plans, but after explaining her reasons, he'd reluctantly accepted Darcy's offer. He'd seemed concerned that she might not be able to handle the full responsibility of his two younger sons as well as keeping up with the chores. Even after she reminded him she had handled things quite well while he and the boys had the flu, he'd insisted on leaving her a list of chores that had to be done daily along with emergency phone numbers.

Darcy eyed her image in the bathroom mirror. Was it her imagination or was it more matronly than before she left L.A.? She combed through her sleep-tangled hair, stopping when she saw a sparkle of silver. She leaned closer, frowning as she inspected the spot. Could it be . . . yes, it was . . . a *gray* hair nestled in the auburn mass. One night as a mother, and already there was a gray hair.

Carefully, she separated it and plucked it. "Ow!" she muttered, rubbing the spot on her scalp. She couldn't remember how many hairs there were growing on a human head, but if things kept going at their current rate, she figured she'd be bald in a few years.

She took her toothbrush and toothpaste out of her overnight bag and had just begun to clean her teeth when Scott came bursting into the bathroom. Darcy whirled around, glad she'd chosen a modest night shirt instead of one of her sexier gowns.

"I gotta have some water," Scott stated, rushing to the lavatory. He pulled up the stopper and turned on the water full force.

Darcy stood to one side, her mouth filled with soapy toothpaste and her toothbrush in her hand as she watched Scott open his fingers and let Sebastian slide into the water that had collected in the basin. Darcy stepped closer and joined Scott as they stared down at the dazed goldfish who lay almost motionless.

"I've never seen him swim like that," Scott said.

Slowly, Sebastian began tipping until he was on his side. Darcy wasn't a fish specialist, but she didn't think the prognosis looked good.

"Why were you carrying Sebastian around?" she managed to ask, wishing she could rinse her mouth.

"I thought he might like to get out of his bowl for a while and go for a walk with me."

"Scott, fish don't go for walks. They have to be in the water to breathe," she tried to explain.

"That's silly. Of course, they breathe air. I've seen the bubbles, and he comes to the top of the bowl all the time."

"Yes, he breathes air, but it has to go through his gills."

"Why?"

Scott gave her a confused look, and she realized she didn't know enough about the actual mechanics of a fish's respiratory system to explain.

"Why didn't you just put him back in his bowl?" she asked, changing the subject.

"'Cause Joe knocked the fishbowl over. But it didn't break," he hurried to add. "It just spilled."

"Great," Darcy muttered, thinking about the mess the water had probably made on the carpet. "Go get the fishbowl and we'll refill it. And then put Joe outside. I don't think your dad likes having your puppy in the house."

"Oh, he doesn't mind."

"Well . . . do it anyway," Darcy insisted, not sure how Luke would react, but knowing the dog would only complicate the cleanup.

Scott ran out of the room and Darcy took advantage of his absence to carefully wash her mouth out, spitting in the toilet. When Scott returned, she refilled the bowl, then picked up Sebastian by the tail and transferred him from the lavatory.

For a few seconds, he remained in a motionless, vertical position. Encouraged because he hadn't immediately gone belly-up, Darcy gave him a gentle prod with the tip of her finger. To her relief and Scott's delight, Sebastian perked up and wiggled off in a sluggish, but horizontal circle. In only a matter of seconds, his swimming had become almost normal.

"Let me finish getting dressed and I'll carry him into your room." Darcy herded Scott toward the door. "Then we'll wipe up the water." She locked the door behind him, then gazed back into the mirror. Was that another gray hair? Two in one day? It would take less time than she thought.

She and Scott cleaned up the mess in his room as much as possible, then they went downstairs for breakfast. Adam volunteered to show what he'd learned in family living class and cooked French toast for all three of them.

Darcy felt a little intimidated that a thirteen-year-old could cook better than she could. "I'm going to fix homemade spaghetti for dinner. Do you think there's any Ragu in the pantry?"

There wasn't, so they made a leisurely trip to town, stopping at the arcade to play a few dollars worth of games after she had bought all the necessary ingredients at the grocery store. After eating lunch at the only hamburger place in town, they made one last stop at a video rental store where they each selected a favorite movie to watch that evening.

They all three worked together to do the chores, finishing just before dark. While the boys played in the living room, Darcy cooked the spaghetti, heated the sauce and warmed up a loaf of garlic bread in the oven. Suddenly, the sound of a crash, followed by a scurrying of feet caused her to drop the pot holder and run to the large family area.

"He did it," Adam declared, pointing at Scott.

"He did it," Scott announced simultaneously, pointing to Adam.

Darcy surveyed the room, looking for whatever had made the noise, then groaned when she saw the picture frame lying on the floor next to a football. Gingerly, she picked it up, being careful to avoid the jagged slivers of glass sticking out from the front.

"Oh no," she lamented when she saw it was the picture of Ellen. Why did it have to be *that* picture? Would Luke think she had broken it on purpose?

"What were you guys doing playing ball in the house? I'll bet your dad doesn't let you do that."

"Oh sure he does," Adam stated, sliding a warning glance at Scott.

"Dad doesn't mind," Scott confirmed, but his bright blue eyes were troubled. "You aren't going to tell him we did it, are you?"

"No, I'll think of something. But you two promise me you won't break anything else while I'm here."

"We promise," they both swore.

Adam sniffed the air. "Is something burning?"

"The bread!" Darcy raced back into the kitchen just in time to save the bread from total destruction. She tore off the top crusts and carefully removed only the spaghetti that hadn't stuck to the bottom of the pan when the water boiled dry. Then she called the boys. They sat down and filled their plates after Adam said the blessing.

"Hey, this is good," Adam told her, reaching for a second helping. "See, you *can* cook."

"That wasn't exactly how my mother makes it," Darcy admitted. "But it wasn't bad, was it?"

There was a smear of sauce on his chin as Scott smiled his agreement that the meal was acceptable.

Darcy tried to remember that her dinner mates weren't the most discerning culinary critics, but she was becoming more pleased with her success as each moment passed.

They rinsed the dishes and loaded the dishwasher before cooking a big bowl of popcorn and settling in front of the TV for a movie marathon.

"Do you guys eat all the time?" Darcy asked, amazed at the amount of food the boys had devoured that day. It was more than she usually ate in a week. But, blaming it on the country air, she'd reached for a handful of popcorn. If she didn't stop, it wouldn't take but a few months before she was bald *and* fat.

They were halfway through a Disney animated movie when the electricity flickered once, then went out. Instantly, the house was smothered in darkness and a spooky silence.

For several long minutes, Darcy, Adam and Scott didn't move or speak. The darkness was so intense they couldn't see each other even though they were sitting only a few feet apart. As Darcy waited for the lights to come back on, her thoughts ran wild with the possibilities of what could have caused the electricity to be cut off.

Of course, extreme weather sometimes brought down power lines, but she didn't think that could be it. While the temperatures outside were in the thirties, it wasn't cold enough for an ice problem. It wasn't snowing and the wind wasn't blowing hard.

Assuming it wasn't something so simple as Luke having forgotten to pay the bill, there had to be a logical explanation. Darcy's imagination began making suggestions she truly didn't want to consider...such as the chance it might not be a *something* that had caused the blackout, but a *someone*. What if a burglar were lurking around outside...or a kidnapper? A criminal might have escaped from a nearby prison or an insane person out of an asylum. The fact that there were neither of these in the general vicinity of Greenhaven made absolutely no difference as Darcy's panic grew.

She felt a hand on her knee, and she nearly jumped over the back of the couch.

"Darcy, I'm not scared of the dark or nothing like that," Scott said in a small voice, "but can I sit on the couch next to you?"

"Sure, Scott, come on up here next to me." Darcy patted the seat cushion. "The lights will be back on any minute now."

Adam didn't ask, but moved up to sit on the other side of Darcy.

It occurred to her that she was responsible for the safety of these two children, which complicated the matter. She had to think quickly and, above all, not show any signs of fear.

"Why don't we all go into the kitchen and call the power company," she suggested. "Adam, do you have any idea where your dad keeps the flashlights or some candles?"

"Sure, I'll get them." Adam stood up, but didn't move away. "Aren't you coming with me?" he asked, trying desperately to sound brave, but not quite succeeding.

"Of course we are. We're going to all stay together until we get some sort of lights working." Darcy took Scott's hand and stood up. Both boys stayed right at her heels as she bumped her way through the living room, across the hall and into the kitchen. Adam took flashlights out of a drawer and handed one to Darcy and one to Scott.

Darcy tried to make it look as if she was randomly shining the light around, but her intent was to see if the lock on the back door was fastened. Out in the country, it was something people usually didn't bother with. But her city instincts must have automatically kicked in, because the door was securely locked. At least someone couldn't simply walk in on them.

*Stop thinking things like that!* Darcy scolded herself. Aloud she said, "Where's the phone book?"

"I'll get it," Scott volunteered with an eagerness that said he was more interested in using the flashlight than he was frightened of the dark. He retrieved the book from a bottom cabinet and took the long way around the kitchen to bring it to Darcy.

She tried not to seem impatient as she took the phone book from him and flipped to the listing. "Shine your lights on the telephone," she told the boys. They complied, but couldn't resist jousting with their light beams. Almost blinded by a stray flash directly into her eyes, Darcy had to squint to focus on the small lettering. Bald, fat and forced to wear bifocals. Darcy was beginning to grow very concerned that she would not survive the evening.

Her fingers had punched out four of the seven numbers when Joe suddenly began barking with a hysteria Darcy couldn't ignore. Her worst fears were coming true. Someone was out there.

"Stay behind me," she ordered Scott and Adam in a voice that would not tolerate disobedience. She crept to the window, pushed the curtain aside and peeked outside. "Oh my God," she gasped and began fumbling with the lock. She jerked the door open and ran outside screaming, "Get away. Go on. Leave Linda alone."

But the mangy coyote stood his ground. Linda dangled limply from his mouth while Joe raced in frantic circles around the wild beast.

Darcy looked around for something to throw at the coyote, but couldn't find anything in the tidy backyard. Scott stood beside her, clinging to the tail of her blouse and sobbing at the sight of his pet. If there was any hope to save the turkey, Darcy didn't have time to comfort Scott. She was making a second search of the yard when Adam came running out of the back door with a .22 rifle in his hands.

"I'll shoot him," Adam announced and was lifting the gun to his shoulder when the coyote lunged at Joe, sending the puppy tumbling backward against the fence. The wild animal whirled and turned to face the people, growling around the bird still in his mouth. With his four feet firmly planted, his eyes glowed yellow in the unsteady beam of Darcy's flashlight and his teeth looked huge and deadly as his upper lip curled back in an angry warning.

Before Darcy could stop him, Scott had released her shirt and was dashing across the yard to where Joe lay whimpering. The coyote lowered his head, watching the little boy with one eye and Darcy and Adam with the other.

Darcy didn't stop to think. She grabbed the gun out of Adam's hands, brought the stock firmly against her shoulder, centered the big coyote in the open sights and squeezed the trigger.

The coyote's mouth opened and Linda tumbled to the ground. He whirled to face Scott as if he was blaming the boy for the sudden pain. He took a step forward, staggered and fell into a lifeless pile on the ground.

Darcy raced over, pausing only long enough to poke the animal with the muzzle of the gun to make certain he was dead, and grabbed Scott into her arms. She hugged the shaken boy tightly against her and felt the hot sting of tears spill down her cheeks. She realized her heart was hammering so wildly in her chest that she couldn't breathe. Her legs wobbled beneath her and she stumbled to the porch before her knees buckled altogether. She sat on the top step, cradling Scott on her lap with Adam kneeling behind her, his hand on her shoulder.

Joe galloped over to the porch and pushed his way onto Darcy's lap. He cocked his head from side to side, apparently sensing that his people were upset and wanting to help them. He offered his best form of support by covering Scott's face with puppy kisses and even giving Darcy a couple of licks on her cheek. His duty done, he tumbled down the steps and ran to where his friend still lay on the ground. He nudged the turkey with his nose and gave her a few barks of encouragement.

Linda, as if realizing she'd played dead long enough, jumped to her feet. She shook herself, then ruffled her feathers and stalked around the fallen coyote, scolding him with angry yelps.

"She's alive!" Scott exclaimed, his tears quickly replaced with a smile. He jumped off Darcy's lap and began playing with his pets.

"Well, Adam," Darcy said, glancing up at the older boy. "We did it. Thanks for your help."

"I could've shot that coyote, too," Adam answered, sounding a little annoyed that he hadn't been the one to save his brother. "How come you know how to shoot so good anyway? I didn't think reporters used guns."

"I didn't learn how to handle a gun because I'm a reporter, although there have been times when I would have felt more comfortable with a rifle in my suitcase," Darcy explained.

A pair of headlights pierced the darkness as a truck turned into the driveway. Darcy was too weak to feel alarmed. In fact, she didn't move from the steps as the truck stopped beside the gate and a man got out.

Adam turned his flashlight toward the man who blinked at the sudden bright illumination. The light reflected off the power company insignia on the door of the pickup truck.

"Good evening, ma'am. I'm Bill Taylor with Greenhaven Light and Power. We're having a little trouble in this area. Is your electricity off?"

Darcy didn't know if she wanted to hug him or slap him. "Yes, it is."

Bill took a high-powered flashlight from the truck and arched its beam around the yard. It halted when it encountered the body of the coyote. "It looks like you had a visitor."

"He was after Linda. She was in his mouth," Scott stated.

"Linda's the turkey," Darcy explained before the man could ask the obvious question. "Would you do us a favor and drag him out of the yard?"

He opened the gate and walked to the dead animal. "He's a big one, probably a dog cross." He bent down and got a good grip on the coyote's tail. "I'll leave him beside the garage. Then I'm going to climb the pole in your front yard and check the transformer. We think it might have blown out."

Darcy nodded mutely, almost overcome with exhaustion and relief. All she wanted to do was to get back inside the house, lock the doors, put the boys to sleep and fall into bed herself. She dared not look into the mirror. She didn't want to see the zillions of gray hairs that had surely sprung up from the night's excitement.

She got the boys to put Linda in her cage where she should have been all along. Then they left Bill to finish his work alone in the dark night.

Darcy was awakened the next morning by the ring of the telephone. She fumbled across the unfamiliar nightstand, knocking off a notepad and pen before finding the telephone.

"Hello," she mumbled, her voice muffled by the pillow.

"Darcy? Is that you?"

Through the mist of sleep still dulling her brain she recognized her attorney's voice.

"Yes, Sheldon. It's me. Just don't ask how I feel."

"I don't have to ask because I know how you'll feel within the next two minutes," Sheldon gushed enthusiastically. "I have some great news!"

# Chapter Fourteen

There was actually a hint of a smile on Greg's face when he and Luke returned late Sunday afternoon. He didn't say anything to Darcy, but, for the first time, he met her gaze without open hostility.

Luke considered that quite an achievement. He hadn't realized his son felt so threatened by the possibility of adding a woman to the Calloway household. Luke had thought because the boys welcomed Nell that they wouldn't mind having a new mother to share their lives.

"How'd it go?" Darcy asked.

Before he answered her, he greeted her with a kiss that wasn't long enough to suit him, but was long enough for Adam and Scott to lose interest in their card game and start staring at the two adults.

"I missed you," he whispered in her ear. "That sleeping bag was so big and empty without you."

"Not as big and empty as your bed was."

He looked down at her beautiful face and wanted to take her to his bed at that very moment. He doubted he would ever tire of making love with her. And he hoped they had the rest of their lives to find out.

Very aware of the three pairs of eyes and ears watching and listening, he went to the kitchen sink, washed his hands and splashed some water on his face. The only running water he and Greg had been around for the past two days had been in an ice-cold stream that had effectively discouraged any bathing. It looked like the chances of being alone with Darcy were slim to none, so he'd settle for a hot shower and a change of clothes. He combed his fingers through his damp hair and asked, "So what did you and the boys do?"

Darcy exchanged a peculiar look with Adam and Scott before answering. "Oh not much. We played games, practiced for the play, revived a goldfish, played football, rented videos, made spaghetti, ate popcorn, shot a coyote, had pancakes for breakfast—"

"Whoa...back up," Luke interrupted. "What was this about a coyote?"

"Darcy shot a coyote, Dad," Scott declared, bouncing up and down in his chair. "Right in the backyard. And he had Linda in his mouth."

"What was a coyote doing in our backyard?"

Scott grimaced and looked down at the table. "Uh...I sort of forgot to put Linda in her cage. Then when the lights went out, we got scared when Joe started barking so we went outside and Darcy shot the coyote. And a man came over in a big truck and climbed up our pole."

Luke felt as if he'd gone for popcorn in the middle of a movie and returned after the most important scene. There was a great deal of information missing from the story he was hearing. He turned to Darcy.

"*You* shot a coyote and a man climbed our pole? What does that mean?"

"Come on and we'll show you." Darcy filled in the gaps as they walked to the side of the garage. "Then after Bill dragged the coyote out here, he had to call a crew out to fix the transformer on the pole at the end of the driveway. The lights still hadn't come on by the time we went to bed, so they must have had to work on it until early in the morning."

They stopped next to the dead animal and Luke studied it in amazement. "Good shot," he said, eyeing the single hole through the coyote's heart.

"I told you I could shoot."

"You also told me you'd never taken a shot at a live target."

"He didn't leave me any other choice." Darcy's tone was genuinely filled with regret. "I tried to chase him away, but he was determined to take Linda with him. Poor thing, he was probably just hungry. But when he went for Scott, I had to do something."

Luke bent down and picked up Scott. He couldn't keep from giving the little boy a tight hug. He didn't know what he'd do if something happened to Scotty. It would be like losing Ellen all over again.

"I know it's not enough, but thanks. I owe you a big one," Luke said to Darcy. "So where's the turkey? There goes our Thanksgiving meal. I guess we'll have to pick out another one even though the turkeys that are left are a few weeks too young."

"Dad! We're not going to *eat* Linda!" Scott exclaimed.

"Not anymore. This coyote could be rabid so we couldn't eat anything he killed."

"But he didn't kill her," Adam informed him.

"She played dead," Darcy added. "And she's so fat that he couldn't close his mouth enough to bite through her feathers."

"We're not going to eat *Linda,* are we, Dad?" Scott repeated with growing concern.

"We'll talk about that later," Luke said, anxious to avoid the subject as long as possible. Sooner or later Scott would have to face reality. But not now. "Did you say the coyote bit Joe, too?"

"No, but I think he might have caught him with his claws. Joe had a couple scratches on him," Darcy explained.

"Then I'll have to take the coyote in to the county agent and have him checked for rabies. The puppy's still too young to be in danger, but we'd better be sure." He continued to gaze down at the big, mangy animal. "We saw a lot of pheasant hens, but no roosters. You shot more than we did."

"I'm not proud of that," Darcy stated. "I just did what I had to do."

"We'll make a day of it tomorrow. I'll drop the coyote off, then I'll take you to lunch before we go to the school for Scott's play."

"I . . . uh . . . I've got something to tell you," Darcy said. She looked up at him. Her expression was excited, but edgy.

A cold feeling of dread washed over him. Before she even spoke, he knew he wasn't going to like her news. He put Scott down and patted him on the back. "Why don't you take Joe and the turkey to one of the empty barns. They'll have to stay there until we're sure they haven't been exposed to rabies. And be careful that they don't bite or scratch you.'' He waited until the boy was in the backyard before asking Darcy, ''So when are you leaving?''

''Tomorrow morning. Purity Products dropped their suit, so the police decided not to press charges. Apparently the public mounted a campaign for my return.''

''They want you back,'' he stated flatly.

''Yes, isn't that terrific?'' She was almost bubbling with enthusiasm. ''The station wants me to be there on Wednesday. They're giving me back my co-anchor job.''

Luke wasn't sure what she expected him to say. Surely she couldn't think he'd be glad.

''My mother was disappointed that I wouldn't be here for Thanksgiving, but I told her I'd try to get back for Christmas or at least Easter.''

''Great. Christmas or Easter,'' he repeated dully.

As if it suddenly dawned on her that he wasn't sharing her enthusiasm, her expression sobered. ''I thought I might be satisfied living here in Iowa, but when they offered me my job back...I just have to go. Please understand.'' Her traitorous blue eyes pleaded with him.

''Sure, I understand. Me and the boys were a good way to pass the time until something better came along.''

''That's not it at all.'' Darcy moved forward and reached out to touch him, but he stepped back.

"Luke, I *really* thought it might work between us. I *do* love you. And I'll come back. Maybe we can keep the romance going...."

"No thanks. Don't do me any favors. I'm just a hick farmer. I can't possibly hope to compete with the klieg lights of Hollywood."

"Luke, don't do this. You're not even trying to see my side. I've worked all my adult life to get where I am in the business. I would be foolish to throw it all away. I'm still young. In a few years, maybe I'll be ready for a major change."

Luke squared his shoulders, suddenly feeling exhausted and very old. "Well, don't call me. I won't be waiting."

"I thought you loved me. Please give me some time."

"Take all the time you want."

She heaved a pained sigh. "We're both tired. I'll come over early in the morning before I leave and we'll talk some more."

"Where are you going tomorrow?"

Luke and Darcy whirled around, unaware that Scott had rejoined them.

"I'm going home tomorrow."

"Home? That's not too far away," he responded.

Darcy knelt in front of Scott so they were eye level as she explained, "No, not my parents' home. I'm going back to California tomorrow."

"You're leaving us?" Scott's expression reflected all the pain and shock Luke was feeling.

"I'm not leaving you. I'll be back in a month or two. But I've got to go to work."

"You can work here. We have news."

Luke's smile was bittersweet. How like a child to come up with a perfectly logical solution that would, of course, be unacceptable to Darcy.

"I'm sorry, Scotty, but I have to go back to L.A. That's where my real home is."

"But you're going to miss my play," Scott cried, his big blue eyes filling with tears. "You *can't* miss my play."

Darcy hesitated, obviously torn between her need to begin the long drive as early as possible and her desire not to disappoint the little boy.

"I guess I could leave right after the play and drive until midnight," she mused. "Okay, Scott, I'll be there."

Temporarily appeased, Scott ran back to the yard.

"We could have that lunch," Darcy suggested in her soft, sexy voice. He hated that it still had the power to send his heart rate into overdrive.

"No, I'll be busy all day tomorrow," he retorted harshly. "I forgot about some important errands."

"Can we talk in the morning?"

"No, I think too much has been said already." His jaw was clenched so tightly he thought his teeth might crack from the pressure.

"Luke...please..."

"You're wasting your time in news. You should be an actress," he remarked, wanting to hurt her as much as she was hurting him. "If you need any references for your performance in bed, just tell them to call me. You were good, baby. It was real Academy Award material."

Her hand arced through the air, but he caught it before it connected with his cheek. For a moment they glared at each other. Then he uncurled his fingers from around her wrist and pivoted stiffly. Without a backward glance, he headed for the turkey barns.

He heard the sound of her car door shut, followed by the Corvette's engine roaring to life. Luke stopped when he reached the first barn. He stepped into the shadows and turned to watch her drive away.

As far as he was concerned it would be the last time. She had made her choice. And it didn't include him except as a sort of diversion when and if she found time to take a vacation. He and his boys had been a middle-America Disneyland for a woman who wanted to experience family life as an adventure and not a reality.

But he couldn't blame it all on her. He'd known who she was and how she felt about her career. He'd been foolish to believe she would give up a life of glamour and wealth to become a farmer's wife. He'd been even more foolish to let himself fall in love with her.

Luke's hand clutched the material over his chest as if that would relieve the hurt inside. She had warned him...she *was* a good shot. She'd made a direct hit to his heart. He hoped someday it would heal.

"SURELY THEY WOULD let you stay until after Thanksgiving," Betty pleaded. "We were so counting on having you home for the holidays."

"I know Mother. So was I. But I've missed a month's work and I have bills to pay. You have no idea how high the cost of living is in California."

Her mother gave her an eloquent look that clearly said Darcy wouldn't have that problem if she moved back to Iowa.

"I'm going to leave directly from the school, so I'd better give you all hugs and kisses now." Darcy looked around the room at the dear faces of her parents, her brothers and their families who had all gathered to give her a proper farewell. Although no one voiced the words, they knew this might be the last time they were all together for a long time. Darcy's parents were getting on in years. If as many years lapsed between her next visit as from her last, even her siblings would be approaching middle age. Darcy made the circuit of the room, embracing her family and making promises she knew she might not be able to keep. Betty was making no effort to hide her tears and even J.W. looked unusually misty eyed.

Why were they making this so hard for her? Didn't they want her to be happy? Didn't they want what was best for her? They'd known this was just a visit.

Darcy blinked back a few tears of her own as she slid behind the wheel of her car. It had taken a lot of creative packing to get her suitcases wedged into the small space.

"Call when you get there so your mama won't worry about you," J.W. demanded.

"Be careful," Betty added her own, more gentle command. "We love you, honey."

"And I love you, too. All of you. Take good care of each other." Darcy waved as she turned around in the driveway and headed toward the road. "Goodbye."

It was still early, so she took the long way into town. The fact that it would take her past Wishbone Acres was purely coincidental. The Corvette began to slow as she approached the driveway. Almost automatically, it turned in and pulled to a stop next to the gate.

For several seconds, Darcy sat behind the wheel, trying to decide whether she should go in and try to talk with Luke once more or whether she should wait until he calmed down. She could always call him from L.A. Maybe she could convince him that even though her feelings for him were stronger than for any other man she'd met, she still felt her first responsibility was to her career.

She wanted Luke, but she wanted to be the best newswoman in the business. If she were to give it up now to become a wife and mother, it would be like letting down the entire female population. She would be proving that women couldn't be as dedicated to their careers as men, and that love and marriage were more important than ambition and achievement in the business world.

She had to talk to him. Surely he'd understand. Maybe there was a compromise she just wasn't seeing right now. If what they were feeling for each other was real love, the kind that would last a lifetime, then it could wait a few more years.

Darcy turned off the engine and got out. She didn't see his truck and the coyote was gone, so he probably wasn't even home. As she opened the gate, she missed having Joe and Linda rush out to greet her, but guessed they were probably still in quarantine in the barn.

The back door was unlocked, as usual, and no one answered her knock. Darcy turned the knob and stepped inside. Her heart skittered in her chest at the memory of the last time she had slipped into the house thinking Luke wasn't home.

Perhaps he was upstairs right now, taking a shower, with the warm water trickling down his muscular torso, slowed by the patch of curling hair on his chest...and lower. She imagined that he would turn toward her when she entered the bathroom and his body would react, rising and swelling in anticipation of what would happen as soon as she could remove her clothes and join him beneath the pelting spray. First they would make wild, crazy love, then they would talk.

She hurried up the stairs, wanting to surprise him. The door to his room was closed, but when she opened it, there was no sound of water running in the bathroom. As she stepped inside, she could see the bathroom door was open and no one was there. She let her gaze travel around the room. On the wall next to the dresser was an oil painting of a country landscape she and Luke had bought at an antique store one afternoon last week.

They'd had fun that day, spending the morning in bed and the afternoon in town, exploring all the little stores and having an impromptu picnic in the park. Darcy couldn't remember ever feeling so relaxed and peaceful. It had been a perfect vacation.

Her gaze lingered on the bed. The comforter had been thrown back, clearly showing that only one person had slept there last night. The pillow still showed the imprint of Luke's head. Darcy trailed her fingers across the blue-striped cotton as if it were Luke's dark brown hair, rumpled from their lovemaking and falling across his forehead in a charmingly boyish way. The undershirt he'd slept in was tossed carelessly across the foot of the bed. Darcy picked it up and rubbed its softness against her cheek. The fragrance of soap and Luke's after-shave clung to it, and after only the briefest pause, she hugged it against her and left the room.

Luke's truck was in the parking lot at the school, but he was nowhere in sight. Darcy parked and locked her car, then followed a couple of parents into the elementary auditorium.

The room had been designed to hold about two hundred people, but chairs had been set up for only seventy-five since just the first, second and third grade classes were involved in the program.

Darcy found a seat near the back, so she could slip away as soon as the play was over, and on the aisle so Scott could see she had come to watch him. She glanced around, nodding to several people she knew or recognized from church. Her gaze eventually halted on the back of Luke's dark head where he sat at least a dozen rows in front of her. His hair was neatly combed, its texture so familiar to her that she could almost feel it beneath her fingers. She willed him to look around, but he kept his attention focused forward.

The lights in the auditorium dimmed, leaving only the stage area brightly illuminated. The principal came out, welcomed the parents and guests and presented the introduction to the play.

It was surprisingly complicated for an elementary-school play, beginning when the pilgrims arrived in America on a large cardboard ship and showing them building their houses. Scott was an Indian, so he had only a small part in the beginning of the play. Darcy waited, impatient with the other children's halting delivery of their lines and hoping that Scott would be perfect. When he finally came onstage, she straightened in her chair, watching with a pride that swelled in her chest like an empty sponge soaking up memories.

He was one of the Indian leaders who offered to share their food with the pilgrims. And, to the delight of the other children and the audience, he was carrying Linda.

Darcy could only assume the rabies report had been negative for Luke to allow Linda to participate. Scott had told her he'd asked his teacher if he could bring his pet. With her bronze coloring, Linda resembled her wild ancestors, but her heavy, broad-breasted body was very modern. However, there was no denying that she added to the atmosphere and, unintentionally, the humor.

At last, everyone sat down to dinner, Indians and pilgrims side-by-side. Linda pranced around the stage, pecking at ears of corn that were being used for decoration and the shoestrings of the sneakers that peeked out from under the children's costumes. She wasn't satisfied until the strings were completely untied and dangling loose. Whispers and muffled chuckles rippled through the audience as they watched the turkey's antics and the children who were trying so hard to ignore her. Finally, she jumped up on the table and began eating the cornbread and popcorn off the students' plates.

The children finally finished their lines and stood to take a bow. But as the audience began clapping and whistling their approval, Linda reacted as any turkey would to the sudden loud noise. She panicked.

With a terrified yelp, she spread her wings and tried to lift her butterball body off the table. Instead of flying away like her wild ancestors, her escape became a series of awkward, unpredictable leaps, landing in the audience and jumping with a great flurry of her large wings from one person to another.

The audience's reaction was a mixture of laughter and screams, depending on whose head Linda was standing upon. Luke vaulted from his seat and began chasing the turkey, but that only seemed to frighten her more. With a mighty thrust she managed to launch herself directly toward the door.

Darcy reacted automatically, standing and catching Linda in midair.

"Shh ... calm down, Linda. It's going to be okay ... you're not going to be lunch just yet."

Linda must have recognized the voice because she relaxed against Darcy, becoming almost as limp as when Joe carried her in his mouth. The twelve-pound body suddenly felt like it weighed twice that and Darcy was glad when Luke arrived to relieve her of her load.

"So you made it," he said, his voice cautiously neutral.

"I told Scott I would."

One dark eyebrow arched as if to say he hadn't counted on her to keep her word.

"Darcy, you're here!" Scott pushed his way through the crowd and threw his arms around her waist in an affectionate hug. "How did I do?"

She knelt in front of him. "You were perfect...I was so proud of you."

"You helped me lots." His smile slid away and his blue eyes darkened. "You aren't really going to leave us, are you? Not *really*."

"Yes, I have to. But I'll call and write you letters. Wouldn't you like to have a pen pal?"

He stared at her solemnly. "I'd rather have a mommy."

Darcy couldn't think of a single response. She gave Scott a quick kiss and stood. Over the boy's head she met Luke's gaze and saw the same pain and disappointment that was in Scott's young eyes.

She turned and ran, fleeing...as her pastor had always preached...from temptation.

# Chapter Fifteen

"If you think things are dull here in L.A., there's a bar in Kansas City that allows its patrons to dress in a fuzzy suit and throw themselves against a wall of Velcro," Darcy said, reading the copy on the monitor while a film clip ran behind her.

"I've been throwing myself against walls for years, but I haven't been able to stick. Velcro will be a real improvement," her co-anchor Jason St. James responded and they both laughed.

"And that's the weekend update," Darcy added, looking directly into the lens. "Good night and drive friendly."

She continued smiling until the red light on top of camera two blinked off.

"Good job. It's great to have you back, Darcy," the director called.

"Thanks." She took off the tiny speaker attached to an almost invisible earplug and unclipped the microphone from her silk blouse.

Jason went through the same procedure, then stood up and stretched. "How about dinner? Or do you already have other plans?"

Darcy sighed and massaged the back of her neck. "Sure, dinner sounds fine. I'm getting tired of eating alone at home. Give me a minute to get my purse."

He met her outside her dressing room. "My car is in the shop...again. Would you mind dropping me off at my place after we eat?"

"Not at all. Let's go. I'm starving."

They walked together to the underground parking garage and Darcy unlocked the passenger door before walking around to the driver's side. When she got in, Jason held up a brown feather in front of her face and asked, "What's this? Did you hit a bird?"

"No, that's Linda's."

"Excuse me?"

"Linda is a pet turkey...well, she's actually not a pet. She's going to be Thanksgiving dinner for a family I know in Iowa."

"You let a turkey ride in your car?"

"No, and I have no idea how that feather got in here. It must have been on my clothes after I caught her during the play."

Jason shook his head. "You lost me. It sounds like life in the heartland is as strange as life in L.A."

Darcy reached for the feather, but Jason didn't notice her response as he rolled down the window and tossed the feather outside. She watched in her rearview mirror as the feather swirled, then was lost in the darkness of the night. For an unknown reason, she felt the loss was much more significant than that of a feather on the wind. It was a link with Greenhaven...a link with a family she had grown to love very much...a link with a completely different world.

"So what are you hungry for...Chinese?" Jason asked, oblivious to Darcy's sudden mood swing.

It had been happening a lot during the last few days. She'd arrived to find her house had been burglarized in her absence. Her drawers had been dumped and her televisions, VCRs and stereo equipment, along with what few pieces of expensive jewelry she owned had been taken. Luckily for her and unfortunately for the burglars, she'd never had the time to invest in anything of great value.

Ironically, her neighbors said it had happened the same night that she had been baby-sitting Adam and Scott, worrying about whether or not a burglar might be lurking outside the farmhouse. In Greenhaven they didn't need even cheap locks to keep intruders out while in L.A. her burglars had managed to disarm an expensive security system. But when she thought about it, her loss was nothing when compared to the loss if something had happened to those children.

It dawned on her just how little her things were worth. Oh sure, they had some monetary value. It would cost her insurance company almost twenty thousand dollars to replace what had been taken. But the truth of the matter was, everything she owned could be easily replaced.

They enjoyed a companionable dinner. Jason had made a few passes when she'd first hired on at the station. But Darcy had made it clear she wanted to keep their relationship uncomplicated. Jason seemed almost relieved and they had fallen into a friendship that didn't go beyond a few meals or some out-of-town assignments. But still, as if he felt it was some sort of macho requirement, he always made a half-hearted offer as he did when she stopped in front of his condo.

"Do you want to come in for a nightcap?" he asked.

"No thanks. I'm going to watch a movie and catch the late news."

As she expected, Jason didn't press the issue. "See you Monday."

She drove to her own house and parked her Corvette in the attached garage. She passed through the exercise room to the kitchen, flipping on lights as she went. The darkness had never bothered her before, but somehow now it made the house seem so cold and empty.

She flipped on the new television set in her bedroom and turned on her bath water. After pouring in a generous portion of bath oil beads, she got a nightie out of her drawer and returned to the bathroom.

The hot water lapped against the knotted muscles of her neck and shoulders. She'd forgotten how tense she got when rushing to put together the newscast and prepare for the next day. Actually, she hadn't really noticed it before she left. Maybe the tension had been building slowly through the years. Her stay in Greenhaven had, except for a few incidents, been calm and relaxing, and, contrary to her belief at the time, no new gray hairs had appeared since her baby-sitting escapade.

Her skin was pink when she finally got out of the cooling water. She toweled herself off, then reached for the nightie. But when her hand brushed against

Luke's white T-shirt that was hanging inside her bathroom door, she took it down instead.

She slipped the shirt over her head, sighing with sensual pleasure as the soft cotton material caressed her skin, its hem falling to mid-thigh. She hadn't washed it because its value to her was knowing it had been on Luke's body and still carried his masculine scent.

Returning to the kitchen, she flipped through her mail and tossed it all aside. It was silly to be hoping for a letter with a Greenhaven postmark. Even if someone other than her mother had wanted to write to her, it wouldn't have had time to reach her unless they mailed it Monday evening or Tuesday.

Of course, she could call. She glanced at the clock. Even with the time difference, it wasn't quite eleven o'clock in Iowa. Luke and the boys might still be awake. Maybe they were playing Monopoly or Nintendo. She'd gotten pretty good at a couple of the games, but would never be able to beat Greg or Adam, or even Scott. It was amazing how quick their reactions were.

But no, she wouldn't call them. She'd tried to reach Luke twice after she'd arrived back in L.A., but he had been too "busy" to take her calls. After the second excuse when even Adam couldn't make it sound convincing, Darcy realized it was over between her and Luke. There would be no mending of fences, no waiting, no plans for the future. He'd made his position clear, but she just had refused to listen.

She wished she could be mad at him for his stubbornness or his close-minded attitude toward her work. But she could understand why he could take the stand he did. He'd already made a drastic change in his life, choosing to move from the city to the country. And while he could accept her decision to stay in the rat race, he didn't have to make a place in his life for her to fit should she ever get tired of running. She had to appreciate his honesty and the fact that he wasn't playing games.

And yet, it hurt so badly not to see him or hear his voice. Never would she have believed she could miss a man so much. And his kids . . . she even missed them. She wondered how long it would take to get them out of her mind . . . and her heart.

Monday morning, she joined the other newscasters in their daily meeting. They each took turns explaining a story they wanted to cover or how they planned to handle that day's news. Darcy found herself daydreaming, wondering if Scott had remembered his lunch or if Greg was making a passing grade in algebra.

"Darcy, earth to Darcy, come in please."

Her attention snapped back to the meeting and she felt her cheeks flush hotly when she realized everyone was staring at her with mixed expressions of curiosity and amusement.

"Yes, George. I'm listening," she answered, trying to shrug it off.

"We feel you'd be particularly effective on this assignment. There would be daily reports and then a wrap-up two-hour special when you return next year," the news director explained.

"Uh...where did you say the assignment was?" she asked.

"Russia. We want you to live among the people and see how they're getting along one year after the dissolution of the Soviet Union. You'll travel to all the surrounding countries that were once part of the U.S.S.R. and report on their independence."

"It's a great assignment," Jason commented. "If it wasn't for the play-offs and the Super Bowl, I'd be envious of you getting to spend so much time over there."

Darcy was beginning to wonder just how much of the meeting she'd missed. "How long did you say I'll be in Russia?"

"You'll leave two weeks from today on the thirty-first and come back here the first of March."

"Three months!" she exclaimed. "You want me to stay in Russia for three months. I can't do that."

"I beg your pardon," George stated imperially.

"Darcy, don't be a fool. This is the assignment of a lifetime," Jason whispered. "You could make it to national news on this."

"But I'll miss Christmas and I wanted to be there when they open their presents."

"Be where when who opens their presents?" George asked as he leaned back in his chair and watched Darcy with complete disbelief.

She suddenly realized what she was doing to herself and forced herself to push thoughts of the Calloways out of her mind. "Never mind. It's no big deal. Sure, I'll be ready to go. It sounds like a wonderful assignment. Thanks, George. You won't be sorry you chose me."

"God, you're so lucky," Jason remarked as they left the meeting a half hour later.

"It's not luck," Darcy responded, bristling at the implication. "I've worked hard for this."

"Hey, don't get your hackles up. I just meant that someone up there must be watching over you. After that Earthhope incident, I thought they might be keeping you on a short leash. Instead, they've given you a plum."

"That's because I'm a good reporter."

"Yes, you are. And in a few years when you're sitting in Dan Rather's chair, I hope you'll remember your friends back here in L.A."

Dan Rather's chair. Was that where she wanted to be in a few years? Was that where she wanted to be the rest of her life? To get there she couldn't afford to take time out for a husband or babies. Just look how pregnancy had affected other high-profile female reporters' careers.

But there were those who were able to balance the two. They raised families and were still active in the reporting of the news. Of course, none had achieved the super-anchor status that only ambition and determination could bring. Those positions were all held by men. If she wanted to stay on the course she was on, she knew she might be the first female super-anchor. She could eat, drink and breathe the news, pushing and clawing her way to the top. She could do it.

But at what cost? Did she want to spend the rest of her life alone? Did she never want to hold her own baby in her arms or wake up each morning with the same man next to her in bed? Or did she want to always sleep alone in her own big bed or some hotel room in a different city or even a different country? And she was reminded of the saying that even if a person wins the rat race, they're still a rat.

Somehow Darcy made it through the two newscasts that evening. She was exhausted when she tumbled into bed at midnight. But instead of the blessed relief of sleep, she tossed and turned as her mind wouldn't let the subject go.

By Wednesday afternoon, she knew what she had to do. As she left her house, she knew it wasn't a real home and never would be. She hated its emptiness, its loneliness, its quiet. She wanted to be able to take a deep breath of fresh air and look into the sky at night and see stars instead of police helicopters. She wanted the knots in her shoulders to melt away under the talented hands of her man. She wanted to give Scott a kiss and Adam a hug and tell Greg what a nice kid he was. She wanted to feel a baby of her own kicking inside her and nuzzling at her breast.

And most of all, she wanted Luke.

Her bags were already packed when she went into George's office. She knew it would be next to impossible to get a flight to anywhere within driving distance on the busiest travel day of the year, but she was determined to get there.

She wanted to be home for the holiday.

"George," she began, praying she was doing the right thing, "I want to thank you and the station for standing behind me when I got pulled into that

Earthhope deal. And I want to thank you for considering me for the Russia assignment. Two months ago I would have killed for that job." She paced across the room and stood looking out the window. "But I'm afraid I'm going to have to turn in my resignation...."

THE TAXICAB STOPPED in the driveway and the cabbie jumped out and helped Darcy unload her luggage.

"You were lucky to catch me," the cabbie said. "I was just about to park my cab and have Thanksgiving dinner with my family. If I hurry, I can get back to Omaha before the turkey's out of the oven."

She handed him enough twenty-dollar bills to cover the fare and a generous tip. "I'm glad you were able to bring me all the way here. I would have rented a car, but there weren't any available."

"Hey, this fare was worth it," he said, pocketing the cash. "Have a nice Thanksgiving."

"You, too."

Joe bounced up against the gate, greeting her like a long-lost friend. She gave him a quick pat and a promise for more later. But right now, she wanted to get to the house and see the Calloways.

Even from the yard, she could hear their chatter and their laughter. It was a warm and welcoming sound, something she'd missed more than the fresh air and beautiful scenery.

As she walked up the steps, a case of nerves hit so hard that she had to put down her two suitcases and take several deep, steadying breaths. Finally, she raised her hand and knocked.

"I'll get it," Adam called from inside the house. "Don't start without me."

The door swung open and the surprise registered on his face as soon as he saw her.

"Darcy, I didn't know you were coming today."

"Neither did I, Adam."

"Who is it?" Luke asked, his voice getting closer as he walked toward the back door. When he saw Darcy, there was a flash of pleasure and relief, but he quickly masked his feelings. "When did you get back to town?" He looked past Darcy to the empty driveway. "And how'd you get here?"

She gestured toward her suitcases. "I went to the airport after last night's ten o'clock newscast, and I waited until there was an available seat. I would have flown into any airport within driving distance, but I was lucky to be able to get into Omaha. But then they didn't have any rental cars, so I had to take a cab. I came directly here. My parents don't even know I'm back."

He searched her eyes, trying to interpret exactly what her actions meant. She could see that he was holding back until he knew for sure her intentions.

"I counted my blessings and realized they were all here in Greenhaven," she explained, holding her breath as she watched his expression. "Is it too late?"

He was on the porch and had taken her in his arms before she even realized he'd moved. "Darcy, I love you. I missed you so much. I thought I could be strong, but I want you in my life however I can have you. Even if you want to work in L.A. and fly home for the weekends, we'll work it out."

"I quit my job, but my boss is referring me to a free-lance agency that does special short-term assignments. And if I really want to work, I could apply to take that pregnant newscaster in Des Moines's place at least temporarily." She paused long enough to return his eager kiss. "But what I really want is to take some time off and become part of a special family. I want to get married and have babies. And I might even learn how to cook. Do you know anyone who's looking for a wife?"

"I just happen to be in the market for one myself. Why don't you come inside and you can fill out an application."

Greg and Scott joined them.

"What's the delay?" Greg asked before he could see around his father's broad back. "The pizza's getting cold."

Luke turned and the other two boys saw Darcy. Scott barreled out the door and gave her a big hug. Even Greg seemed glad to see her.

"I got an A on my art project," he told her. "The teacher put it on display on the bulletin board at school."

"That's great," Darcy said, then looked at Luke. "Did I hear that you're eating pizza on Thanksgiving Day? Does this mean Linda got a reprieve?"

"That stupid turkey has become a local celebrity," Luke said with a chuckle. "She made the front page of the *Greenhaven Gazette* the day after the play. We couldn't very well kill her once she got famous."

Linda must have heard her name because she strolled around the corner of the house, peeping contentedly.

Luke wrapped his arm around Darcy's shoulder. "Let's go eat. But first, you'd better call your parents. I hope your mother won't mind you being here instead of with them."

Darcy gave him a knowing smile. "She won't mind. She'll be giving thanks for sure."

"Are you going to stay this time, Darcy?" Scott asked, hanging on to her legs as she walked.

"Yes, Scott. This time I'm here for good."

"For good and forever," Luke added and closed the door behind them.


"OUR PRAYERS HAVE BEEN answered!" Betty exclaimed. "They're going to get married next weekend."

"Luke called and told me the good news," Nell said, her delight obvious even over the long-distance telephone line. "I just knew they were right for each other."

Betty laughed. "Between you and me and the man upstairs, they never had a chance, did they?"

"They should know by now that it pays to listen to their mothers."

"Did I tell you that I've got a new recipe for cherry pies? Wait till next year," Betty promised. "I'll give you a run for your money at the fair."

"I think you'll have the competition all to yourself because I plan on taking a long cruise. Maybe you and J.W. will come with me. Now that my sister's better and we have all our kids settled, we can start living our own lives. I'm even considering buying a cute little town house here in Des Moines."

"Are you kidding? I've got to stick around and start working on Darcy to have me a grandbaby," Betty remarked, already thinking of a plan of action. "And I'm going to help her learn how to cook again and start clipping coupons for her. My work's just begun."

Nell laughed. "The Lord does work in mysterious ways, doesn't He?"

**HARLEQUIN**
*American Romance*®

## ABOUT THE AUTHOR

Kathy Clark grew up on the Gulf Coast of Texas, so she didn't have any hills to go over or woods to go through to get to Grandma's house. But that didn't make their traditional Thanksgiving dinners there any less special.

Kathy says, ''Now that my Grandma has gone (and I'm certain she's baking wonderful cakes up there and making the cherubs ever fatter) and we've moved to Colorado, leaving most of our family behind, our traditions have changed. Last year we went back to Texas (over hills and through woods!) where we had a wonderful time with my husband's relatives (thanks, Pat and Jerry) and enjoyed a delicious meal of . . . yes, turkey. Then with football on television in the background, we played card games until we couldn't put off cleaning up the traditional turkey-day mess any longer.

''From my family (and the Calloway and Carson clans) to yours, may you have a warm, happy Thanksgiving Day with those you love.''

KCCOR

# H A R L E Q U I N

## *A Calendar of Romance*

Our most magical month is here! December—thirty-one days of carolers and snowmen, and thirty-one nights of hot cider and roaring fires. Come in from the cold, get cozy and cuddle with a Christmas cowboy and snuggle with a magic man. Celebrate Christmas and Hanukkah next month with American Romance's four Calendar of Romance titles:

#465
A CHRISTMAS
MARRIAGE
by Dallas Schulze

#466
A COWBOY
FOR CHRISTMAS
by Anne McAllister

#467
SWEET LIGHT
by Judith Arnold

#468
A COUNTRY
CHRISTMAS
by Jackie Weger

Make the most romantic month even more romantic!

COR12

## HARLEQUIN ROMANCE®

**Harlequin Romance
has love in
store for you!**

Don't miss next
month's title in

## THE BRIDAL COLLECTION

### A WHOLESALE ARRANGEMENT
by Day Leclaire

**THE BRIDE** *needed* the Groom.
**THE GROOM** *wanted* the Bride.
**BUT THE WEDDING** was *more* than
a convenient solution!

Available this month in
The Bridal Collection
Only Make-Believe
by Bethany Campbell
Harlequin Romance #3230

Available wherever Harlequin books are sold.

## HE CROSSED TIME FOR HER

Captain Richard Colter rode the high seas, brandished a sword and pillaged treasure ships. A swashbuckling privateer, he was a man with voracious appetites and a lust for living. And in the eighteenth century, any woman swooned at his feet for the favor of his wild passion. History had it that Captain Richard Colter went down with his ship, the *Black Cutter,* in a dazzling sea battle off the Florida coast in 1792.

Then what was he doing washed ashore on a Key West beach in 1992—alive?

**MARGARET ST. GEORGE** brings you an extraspecial love story this month, about an extraordinary man who would do anything for the woman he loved:

### #462 THE PIRATE AND HIS LADY
### by Margaret St. George

*When love is meant to be, nothing can stand in its way... not even time.*

Don't miss American Romance
#462 THE PIRATE AND HIS LADY.
It's a love story you'll never forget.

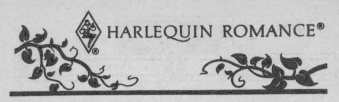

# HARLEQUIN ROMANCE®

After her father's heart attack, Stephanie Bloomfield comes home to Orchard Valley, Oregon, to be with him and with her sisters.

*Orchard Valley*

Steffie learns that many things have changed in her absence—but not her feelings for journalist Charles Tomaselli. He was the reason she left Orchard Valley. Now, three years later, will he give her a reason to stay?

"The Orchard Valley trilogy features three delightful, spirited sisters and a trio of equally fascinating men. The stories are rich with the romance, warmth of heart and humor readers expect, and invariably receive, from Debbie Macomber."

—Linda Lael Miller

Don't miss the Orchard Valley trilogy by Debbie Macomber:

VALERIE   Harlequin Romance #3232 (November 1992)
STEPHANIE   Harlequin Romance #3239 (December 1992)
NORAH   Harlequin Romance #3244 (January 1993)

Look for the special cover flash on each book!

Available wherever Harlequin books are sold.   ORC-2